Halfway to Hell

Gabe Ronan came back to Paradise Valley after seven years hard time in Purgatory Penitentiary. However, he wasn't expecting to be welcomed back with the sight of masked men and six guns tangling with a sheriff who was mighty tough on ex-jailbirds, or the news that his old pard Johnny Keyes now owned half the valley.

But Keyes wasn't the only one of the old bunch still around. They all had guilty consciences and wouldn't believe that Gabe hadn't come back for revenge. And as they started dying one by one, the finger – and the smoking gun – pointed at only one man.

Halfway to Hell

Jake Douglas

A Black Horse Western

ROBERT HALE · LONDON

© Jake Douglas 2006
First published in Great Britain 2006

ISBN-10: 0-7090-7951-6
ISBN-13: 978-0-7090-7951-4

Robert Hale Limited
Clerkenwell House
Clerkenwell Green
London EC1R 0HT

Typeset by
Derek Doyle & Associates, Shaw Heath.
Printed and bound in Great Britain by
Antony Rowe Limited, Wiltshire.

CHAPTER 1

JAILBIRD

They must have stepped aboard the labouring train right at the top of the grade, hiding in brush beside the track until it drew level.

He had heard the straining beat of the loco as it reached the top of Pierce's Peak: this would be where they had jumped on board. Then the train accelerated, slowly at first, gained momentum as the grade steepened on the far side.

The first anyone knew of the three robbers was when the rear platform door crashed open and a shot was fired into the car roof, a man yelling, 'Co-operate, folks, and no one gets hurt! Give trouble and somebody dies!'

It caused panic, shouting, one or two screams from the females. Ronan twisted in his seat, seeing the three bandanna-masked gunmen, the middle one with the smoking gun. His row of seats was almost halfway down the car. Two of the robbers had

5

already started about their business.

A fat man, wheezing, handed over a bulging wallet, his eyes staring wide, sweat sheening his face, jowls a'tremble. The robber dropped the wallet into a gunny-sack he carried, moved on to the next passenger. This was a tall young *hombre*, in clean though faded range-clothes and he wore a sixgun. He handed over a thin roll of notes with his left hand and dropped his right to his gun-butt, in a stupid, careless move.

The robber shot him without hesitation and as the thunder of the shot died this started more screams. The tall ranny crumpled and the robber actually stood on the quivering body to reach the handbag of the fainting woman seated alongside.

The second robber was moving among the rows of seats across the aisle. He gunwhipped an old man – Ronan didn't see any reason for it – and when the young kid alongside, maybe the oldster's grandson, protested, he earned a backhanded blow from the sixgun in the middle of the face. Another female passenger fainted and slid to the floor.

These fellers play rough, Ronan told himself. *More than rough, looked to him like they were deliberately caus- ing terror. Why? There were only about twenty passengers in this the only people-carrying car on the long train. If they were after an express box, they were looking in the wrong place.*

Another man was shot before a masked bandit faced Ronan and said, 'Turn out your pockets, saddle-tramp!'

Ronan knew he looked like a drifter down on his

6

luck. His clothes were old and wrinkled, loose on him in parts, tight in others. His wrists had developed these past seven years so that he could no longer button the cuffs. The sleeves themselves were a couple of inches short, too. His hair under the battered hat – one they had found for him seeing as his own had long since been snatched up by one of the guards because of its newness – was still short and spiky. But he was clean-shaven, a strange feeling after all those years of beard and stubble clogged with dirt and lice.

'Well, friend, don't look to me like you're gonna contribute much to our cause,' the masked man said.

Ronan stiffened.

The man's eyes above the mask were slitted, boring into him hard, roaming up and down his rangy body, almost as if *identifying* him! Ronan felt the knotting twist in his guts, cleared his throat.

'Ain't got but about seven bucks.'

The masked man snorted, flicked his gaze to the other two robbers. 'Hear that? *Seven bucks* is all he's got!'

'Dollar a year,' the one by the door said and his eyes, too, bored into Ronan, taking in his hawk-like profile. Out of the corner of his eye, Ronan saw the man give a slight nod. 'Make sure.'

'Told you to turn out your pockets!' the robber said, cracking Ronan across the ribs with his gun barrel and noting the man was not wearing a firearm. 'C'mon!'

Ronan showed the crumpled paper money and the man slapped it from his hand with a snarl. 'Your pockets, damnit! C'mon *c'mon*, empty 'em I said!'

Every eye in the car, strangely silent now except for the shouting of the robbers and the occasional sob from the one woman passenger who had not yet fainted, was upon Ronan. He had little. A kerchief, a clasp knife with the point broken off by the guard who had handed it to him with his few other belongings, a tin watch that no longer worked – *why did he bother keeping that?* – and a few cents, which the robber knocked from his fingers.

'That paper in your shirt pocket,' the robber snapped. 'Lemme see it.'

Ronan didn't want to: for some reason he had the notion they already knew who he was anyway. It was folded and sweat-damp, greyish, some of the ink smeared. The robber snatched at it and Ronan heard him chuckle behind the bandanna.

'Well, well, well.' He lifted his gaze to the man standing by the door. 'We got us a jailbird here! Travellin' on a ticket issued by the Territorial Correction Centre at Purgatory, Colorado. This here feller's been halfway to hell.'

'Send him all the way,' chuckled the man by the door and there was an explosion that drowned out a scream and a startled curse or two as the robber's big body twisted and crashed into the door, one shoulder going through the glass panel.

Ronan brought up the smoking gun he had ripped from the careless hand of the man in front of him and rammed it into his midriff, stared into the widening eyes and dropped the hammer, twice. The shots were muffled and the robber's body, convulsing, was thrown back over the next row of seats. Ronan twisted down to one knee and triggered at the remaining robber.

The man snapped a shot at him, and again, wild, panicky shots, then turned, snarling, and grabbed the woman who had so far resisted passing out but who now seemed on the verge of doing just that. His arm went about her and clasped her in front of him.

Ronan leapt over the seats as passengers dropped to the floor, everyone shouting.

He stepped over two rows and the man at the door, wounded but still alive, came around, swinging up his gun. He fired and Ronan staggered as lead seared across his side, snapped a return shot that took the robber just beneath the throat.

The hat of the man holding the woman fell off and Ronan saw he was red-haired. Ronan fired at him as he heaved the dead robber away from the door and stumbled out on to the platform. The train was speeding downslope now, the engine way up ahead of a dozen open freight-cars and a caboose in the middle. No one up there could have heard the shooting and being mostly a freight train there was no emergency stopping-cord hooked up to the single passenger car. Splinters flew from the door edge behind him and he turned to trigger but the hammer fell on an empty chamber.

The redhead flung the limp woman from him and came charging towards the door, firing again. Ronan glimpsed the edge of the trees and the gravel embankment, both blurs as the train sped by. If he stayed, he was dead. If he jumped, he could still be dead. Like the robber had said – halfway to hell – but he was a lot closer to it at this moment than he had been in the Territorial Prison all those years.

The redhead had produced a second pistol and Ronan didn't hesitate. Holding one hand against his bleeding side, he tore open the gate in the low fence at the edge of the platform and jumped. The train whipped away from him and he seemed to be suspended in mid-air for a few moments, although the trees and embankment were still blurred.

Suddenly, he fell and he hit the bank feet first, grunted aloud as his knee seemed to be driven up under his chin. Then he somersaulted and the world went crazy, out of kilter, spinning and crashing, tree-tops streaking across the sky, bright flashes behind his eyes. Thudding, hard blows to his body and head and limbs. Breath roaring in gusts from his open mouth.

Almost like being caught in a stampede he thought but swiftly turned his mind away from that. Stampedes were things he didn't allow himself to think about these days, not under any circumstances.

Strange, having such thoughts as he was hurtling down the slope, rolling and bouncing, out of control, unable to stop or take charge of his slide or its direction. Then brush rushed at him and he no sooner threw his arms across his face before branches were tearing at him, ripping his old clothes, scarring whatever flesh was exposed, digging him hard in the body like blunt knives – or a warder's billy, his brain yelled at him, and there never was any escape from *that*, only by way of oblivion.

And it was the same here. Blackness, sudden and

solid, shot through with pain, *plenty* of pain, slammed into him like a solid wall.

The pain was a lot worse when consciousness started to return. His body ached and twitched and stabbed and burned. But he'd had a lot worse these past seven years: his back was a mass of snake-like scars to prove that. The Chief Warden, who liked to be called 'Attila', had a whole set of punishments to fit the 'crimes' as he saw it when inmates didn't conform to his strict rules.

There was a 'Whipping Schedule' from a minimum of five lashes to fifty. Ronan had got as high as twenty-two once and Attila didn't count a stroke unless the lash whistled loud enough for him to hear it where he stood watching from a window in his office across the quad. His ribs had been laid bare.

Yeah, well, that was pain that would stay with him for the rest of his life, he figured: just thinking about it brought it all back to a certain degree, brought the cold sweat squeezing from his pores, put a tremble in his hands and a raw twitching cringe in his back muscles.

The pain he was now experiencing was more immediate but he knew he could stand it. The bullet had gouged across the soft flesh covering the muscle between his hip and the bottom of his rib-cage. Plenty of blood but no real damage, though he knew the wound was deep enough to be sore for quite a while. His legs and arms were lumpy with bruises, scarred with deep scratches from the branches. Blood trickled from a cut above his right eye and one ear felt as thick as a sock and he couldn't hear very well on that side. His hat was gone but he didn't bother looking for it.

He sat for a time, seeing the train way down on the flats on the run into Paradise Valley. He must have been out for no more than ten minutes. Well, Providence wasn't all that far. The country looked pretty much the same as he recalled it, although the railroad had only just started building when he was last here. All he had to do now was follow the tracks.

Not too close, mind, in case that red-haired son of a bitch had jumped, too, and was still looking for him.

Now why did he say 'still'?

He knew why: they had come on to that train to get him. The little dumb act about finding the jail-issue travel voucher was just that – an act. They had been looking for him and the man whose gun he had snatched and killed had been ready to kill him: that was clear enough. The man had said Ronan had spent the last seven years 'halfway to hell' in prison and the one on the door had said: 'Send him all the way.'

But why?

He had done his time, tight-lipped as a beaver's ass, mentioned no names, hadn't told them one thing more than he had done at the trial – and that was nothing. Nothing at all. They were so frustrated that the prosecuting attorney, that smug son of a bitch they'd brought in from Denver, had even offered him a deal: 'C'mon, son, you're what? Twenty-two, twenty-four? You don't want to die young as that.'

12

He winked before continuing. 'Too much living to do yet, boy.' He'd playfully punched Ronan on the shoulder then, grinned without humour. 'Lotta fine women out there, lot of booze if you're so inclined, lot of *living*! Boy, here's a deal for you: name names for me and I'll have you out in under two years, oh, maybe on six months' parole, but you'll be outta that hell-hole and after the six months, free as a bird. What d'you say, boy? It's that or hard-time for life. Maybe a noose.'

Ronan had said what he had said all along – nothing.

Inside, tough guards had tried to make him talk, too, half-killed him a couple of times, but he had long-since grown stubborn and never said a word: took his punishment close-mouthed and accepting his lot. He was surprised when they cut a few months off his sentence, surprised but not complaining.

There must be a reason, but if it was just to kill him, why hadn't they made a real effort in jail and finished the job where they could've covered it up much more easily?

The hell with it. He wanted to get back to Providence, see how the town – and the valley – had grown in seven years. See his old friends, or would they still be friends? Maybe they wouldn't want to know him?

Such things filled his thoughts and he suddenly realized it was almost dark and he had reached the bottom of Pierce's Peak. There was a stream and he splashed into it, letting the chill water soothe his aches and pains. He had no means of making a fire, no food, not even tobacco. So he found a small cutbank and curled up, dragging flood-rack over him for warmth.

It was a bad night, bad as most of them in jail, the pain waking him frequently, chasing the tail ends of heart-pounding nightmares.

But he rolled out at first light, dusted himself down, sluiced his head and face in the cold water, and started off for the valley, away from the railroad tracks now. He knew where he was and could find his way through the pass and on into the town easily. The wound was stiff and painful, had bled during the night.

He had only been walking for twenty minutes when a horseman came out of the brush and blocked his path.

Swaying with fatigue and hurting, he stopped, squinted up at the rider who had placed himself so he was against the early sun. But Ronan saw enough to make out the glint of something on the shirt-front.

'You'd be Gabe Ronan,' the man said in a deep voice. 'You dunno me; I came to Providence after they took you off to jail. Name's Jake Gant, Sheriff.' Then the man's hand lifted and Ronan tensed as the gun hammer snapped back to full cock and the barrel pointed squarely at the middle of his chest.

'You're in a lot of trouble, Ronan. You can come along quietly, or I can shoot you where you stand.' He grinned tightly, briefly. 'See if I can guess which one you'll choose, huh?'

CHAPTER 2

HE'S BACK!

At least it was a bigger cell than the one he had lived in for seven years in Purgatory – no one he knew ever pronounced it '*Purg-a-twar*' although it was spelled that way, 'Purgatoire'.

Jake Gant was a big man of thirty, thick through the body, long-legged, looked as solid as a whiteoak and had a rugged but not unhandsome face. His eyes were unnerving: they bored deep into a man, seeming to get in there amongst his hidden thoughts. But the wide mouth with the heavy lips moved in a half-smile, mocking, confident like most big men who never really expected much resistance to their will.

'Doc says that wound's gonna give you gyp for a spell, but he's got it stitched, so you show some sense and don't go gettin' into too many fights – or jumpin' out of fast-movin' trains – for a spell and you'll be all right.'

Gabe Ronan had been allowed to clean up some

and Gant had even found him reasonable-fitting clothes amongst those in the jailhouse slop-chest, including a hat.

So Ronan was feeling a lot better than when the sheriff had first picked him up, threatened him at first, but then had relented and said, 'Aw, hell, you look plumb tuckered. C'mon, climb on up behind.'

Gant turned out to be a cautious man, too: when Ronan had finally settled on to the horse's rump behind the sheriff, he found that the man had rammed his sixgun into the front of his belt, instead of holstering it where Ronan might be tempted to make a grab for it.

In the town, which Ronan hadn't taken in much, half-asleep as he slouched against Gant's wide back, a sawbones had been called in and then he had been allowed to clean up and dress in better clothes.

Now he was being fed a late breakfast, which he devoured ravenously, hoping his stomach wouldn't rebel at the best food he'd had in seven long, long years.

He was in a cell, but the door wasn't closed.

Gant lounged there now as Ronan ate. 'Grub not much in Purgatory, I guess.'

'Not much. We had a couple cur dogs turn up their noses at leftovers, give you some idea.'

Gant smiled, rolling a cigarette. 'I've heard that. They sent word you were comin' on that train, passengers told me right away you'd jumped off and wanted me to organize a posse to look for you. They figure you for some kinda hero, takin' on them robbers.'

16

Ronan glanced up, said nothing.

'No explanation?'

'What's to explain? They were gonna kill me. I saw a chance and took it. It was self-preservation, not heroics.'

Gant was sober now. 'Queer thing to say – reckon three masked robbers were just there to kill you? A little profit on the side? I'd have to wonder why you'd say such a thing.'

'You weren't there. If you had been, you'd know it's true.'

'Well, I know the two dead ones, local trouble-makers, do anything for a fast buck as long as it didn't entail any work. Usually hung out with a feller named Red Abbott.'

'I winged a redhead. He was still alive and shooting when I jumped.'

Gant nodded several times. 'I'll get lookin' for him – know some of his hang-outs – but, Ronan, seems to me like that dumb trio just got the notion to rob that passenger car, it being so far from the loco, out of the way so to speak.'

Ronan shrugged again, didn't speak, washed the last of the food down with his coffee. Gant studied him thoughtfully, tossed him tobacco sack and papers and, when he had rolled a smoke, flicked him a vesta. Ronan lit up and nodded his thanks through the first exhalation of smoke.

'Looked up your records when I heard you were comin' here, bit of a hell-raiser when you were younger.'

'Just feeling my oats, same as any other young

cowpoke trying to settle down after the war.'

'Yeah, but the war'd been over for three, four years. You were not only feelin' your oats but kickin' the hell outta 'em. You and a wild bunch of friends.' Gant's eyes steadied. 'Went through the war together, eh?'

'We dodged a few Yankee bullets and cannon balls, stayed together after. We just sort of drifted. Ended up here in Paradise Valley. It was just opening up, plenty of work.'

'Yeah, you all didn't seem to mind workin'. It was *after* workin' hours when you got into trouble. High kickin', brawlin', whorin', hard drinkin', lotta ex-soldiers did that they say, tryin' to forget what they'd seen and done or had done to them. Some folk might even say it was almost natural.'

Ronan had nothing to say to that.

'Others'd say you were just a bunch of wild assholes who needed draggin' down a step or three. It's the way I'd've looked at it if I'd been sheriff then.'

'We weren't all that bad. Not by our lights, least-ways.'

'The others'd be the ones were with you when that kid died in the stampede while you were stealin' cows, eh?'

Ronan still said nothing. Gant grinned crookedly.

'Ah, well, you wouldn't name 'em at your trial, so why would you tell me now, huh?' Gant frowned slightly. 'Can't figure why you took all the blame.'

'Was my doing.'

'Nah, you couldn't've done it alone. You had help, but you were the one got caught when your hoss stepped in that gopher hole. Must've been mighty good friends . . . or mebbe not! A really *good* pard would've come forward and taken his share of the blame. 'Stead, the others let you take it all, but you still wouldn't spill the beans.'

'Save your breath, Gant, I ain't gonna get riled or tell you anything.'

'No, guess not. Anyways, you've done your time. Now you're back, and in my town. That's the thing you need to remember: *my* town. You got any notion about gettin' back at these fellers who let you go to jail for them, you forget 'em right now. Savvy?'

'I'm not after anyone's scalp, Gant. I came back to look up old friends, maybe get a job, or a piece of prove up land to settle on here in the valley.'

Gant's eyes narrowed. 'Sure you did. But I'll believe it when I see it. Man tough as you, Ronan, don't strike me as the kind who'll just forget what was done to him.'

Ronan stood stiffly. 'Whatever was done to me, I did to myself, sheriff. Am I free to go?'

Jake Gant had to think about that. 'OK. Now I've been square with you, Ronan—'

'And I'm obliged.'

'You play square with me and both of us'll be happy. I don't need to say no more'n that, do I?'

'Reckon not. I had seven dollars and maybe thirty-odd cents when I boarded the train. I guess you recovered what money the robbers left behind. Can I have what I'm due? I need to hire a horse.'

'Goin' right into the valley, huh?'

'I don't feel like walking.'

19

'Yeah, OK. C'mon through to the front and I'll give you your money. Take your word for how much was took.'

But when Ronan stepped out of the cell he stopped dead. There was a man in dusty range clothes standing in the passage. Gant hadn't been aware of him either, it seemed, by the way the sheriff dropped a hand to his gun-butt.

The man grinned through his gritty stubble.

'Howdy, Gabe, heard you were back. Brung in a spare hoss. Figured you'd want to ride into the valley and see your old friends. Johnny's lookin' forward to it.'

Gant glanced at Ronan who was frowning at the newcomer, squinting. 'Chip? That you? Chip Allard.'

The cowboy sauntered down, smiling slowly, thrusting out his right hand, nodding briefly to Gant.

'Welcome back, Gabe, place ain't been the same without you.'

'And it better not be like it was when he was here before,' Gant growled as the two men shook hands.

He couldn't believe the change in Paradise Valley.

Ranches and farms were dotted all over the place. There was a small dam in the high reaches of Gabriel Creek, feeding the bottom land where lush farm crops grew and green grass spread across the slopes and flats, dotted with browsing cattle.

Forking a sorrel branded with a lone key, Gabe Ronan pushed back the replacement hat Gant had supplied and scratched at his bristly hair. 'I guess by the brand that the hoss belongs to Johnny Keyes,

20

Chip, but all this land his? From the creek, through the woods and up the slopes that fall down on to Deacon Plains?'

'All Johnny's,' confirmed Allard, watching Ronan closely. Chip was about Ronan's age, a year or two older maybe, built lean and muscular like a mountain wolf with ash-coloured hair worn shoulder-length. He had a squint in the left eye and there was a deep, short scar on the cheek below the socket, long ago made by a Yankee spur-rowel.

'Johnny's got a piece of the Hotspurs, too,' he added, bringing Ronan's head around sharply. 'I'm ramrod.'

'For Johnny Keyes?'

Allard smiled. 'Biggest rancher in the Paradise: when the railroad came, it cut across a lot of that land Johnny had title to. Made him rich.'

Ronan looked around him and shook his head slowly. 'I should've stuck around, listened to Johnny when he wanted me to register some of the free range in my name. I'd be better off than I am now.'

Allard sobered. 'Gabe, we're all obliged for what you did. None of us'll forget it, least of all Johnny, you'll see. If you'd named us as bein' in on that rustlin' prank, we'd've all been growin' grey and decrepit on some damn prison rockpile. Or swingin' in the breeze from a cottonwood.'

Ronan looked at him, nodded slightly. 'We all took an oath, remember, Chip? I'd've expected the same from you if you'd been the one got caught.'

Allard squirmed a little. 'Gabe – I – we none of us really expected to have to stand by that oath. Hell, I mean we were just a bunch of young hellions, livin' out a fantasy, ridin' the edge of the Law, nothin' too bad. None of us took that oath real serious, though. It just made us feel good. Growed-up, you know.'

'When Owen got killed in the stampede, and I was caught, it became *damn* serious, Chip.' There was no trace of levity in Ronan now and Allard squirmed some more. 'It was no longer a prank just to stir up the Dawsons and the snooty folk who figured they were *really* living in Paradise.'

'Yeah, well, like you say, it was a prank and we'd had a mite too much moonshine and we all just scattered. Din' know you were down and knocked out, or that Sheriff Mayne would find you near Owen's body.'

'You all lit out for the hills, as I recall.'

'Aw, Gabe! What the hell would you've done? We knew we were in real trouble if we were caught. Old Man Dawson would want to see us strung up. He damn near got you swingin' at the end of a rope, dunno why he just let 'em put you away for seven, eight years. Maybe you're lucky he died while you were away.'

'It's done, Chip,' Ronan said suddenly, his tones clipped, face set in angular lines that gave him an appearance like a hawk swooping in for a kill. 'Finished.'

'You mean that, Gabe?' He waited but didn't get an answer, only a straight, penetrating look. 'Well, what you aim to do? Now you're back.'

Ronan smiled crookedly. 'Aaah! Now I see: Johnny sent you in to sound me out, eh? He's the one with the most to lose if it turns out I'm on the prod, want my pound of flesh from the fellers who ran out and left me to face the music.'

Allard didn't deny it. His hard grey eyes held Ronan's blue-green gaze steadily. There was no levity in him now. 'I asked you what your plans are, Gabe!'

Chip had always been a tough hombre, Gabe recalled.

'Like I told Gant: get a job, or prove up on a quarter-section, settle down. Thinking about Paradise Valley was all that kept me going sometimes in Purgatory, Chip.'

Allard nodded, still sober. 'And now you're back in the valley. With all your old pards livin' hereabouts wonderin' just what in *hell* you're up to!' His face tightened. 'I guess you ain't about to tell me right now, but I have to tell *you*, Gabe, we've all done some growin' up these past seven years. We all have *somethin'* to lose.'

Ronan merely looked at him, more predatory than ever, and Allard smothered a low curse.

'Yeah! Hell, I guess you had to grow up, too, Gabe! More so than us, if you wanted to survive.'

'That was the choice you had in the pen, Chip: do whatever you had to, to survive or die.'

'Well, you obviously did all the right things!'

'You wouldn't want to know what I had to do to stay alive in there, Chip, you or any of the others who stayed here and made good, clean lives for yourselves.'

Chip Allard found his mouth was suddenly dry and there was a feeling in his belly like someone had filled the cavity with half-a-mile of knotted rope.

Was this some kind of a warning, from Gabe Ronan? Chip swallowed. *He's back, all right – but just what the hell is he planning? He had a real grievance and he sure wasn't the same reckless, hell-raising kid he was when he left. He'd gone away a tough kid, and come back looking like a killer!*

There were a lot of people in the valley with plenty to lose if Ronan was aiming to square things for what had happened to him in that Purgatory prison. *A helluva lot!*

Chip figured he wouldn't be the only one who wasn't pleased to see Ronan back in Paradise.

He could too easily turn it into hell.

CHAPTER 3

OLD PARDS, NEW ENEMIES

Johnny Keyes sure looked the part of a rich rancher, thought Ronan as he slowly climbed the log steps leading to the door of the big ranch house where Keyes waited.

The man was smoking a cheroot, watching Ronan warily, likely not even listening to Chip Allard's chatter.

'What you think of this ranny, eh, Johnny? Looks at least ten years older, don't he? And tough as Cochise with a bellyache. Lookit that face! Nose more like a hawk than ever, eyes could double as bullets. But, *there*! The old grin! Just the same as ever. Ah, knew they'd never break Gabe Ronan!' Then he smiled crookedly and added, 'For which we are truly thankful, Lord, unless I miss my guess!'

'You talk too much, Chip,' Keyes said in an easy-listening voice, thrust out his right hand as he stuck the burning cheroot between his teeth and grinned around it. 'Damn good to have you back, Gabe! *Damn* good!'

'I'll hold on giving an opinion on that, Johnny. But you look well. You've thrived since I last saw you.'

Keyes was an average-sized man, but heavy through the shoulders and he had big hands with prominent knuckles. When he hit a man it would be like taking a blow from a knotted branch. His skin was tanned, showing some pockmarks on one side of the neck from shrapnel caught at Manassas. His nose was slightly crooked, and the bright blue eyes looked more like chips of ice than a robin's egg. They narrowed slightly now at Ronan's words and there was a little wariness in Keyes' tone when he answered.

'Told you this place was gonna boom, told all of the old bunch, but no one listened.' He broadened his grin and spread his arms. 'Whatever you see from this porch, and a lot more you can't see because of the mountains, belongs to me. You fellers were too busy having yourselves a high time while I was working. And look where it got *you*.'

Allard stiffened, looked quickly at Ronan who merely shrugged. 'I'll put it down to experience.'

Keyes laughed. 'Still quick with the comebacks, I see, Gabe! Well, long as you learned something.'

'Maybe. At least I won't make the same mistake again.'

That tightened the smile on Keyes' face and Allard stiffened. Ronan turned and looked around across the large yard with its four corrals, two barns, a smithy, some enclosed stables and two stonewalled wells: the nearest to the house had pipelines running under the log and stone walls and Ronan figured there would be a hand-pump in the kitchen. The second well was near the bunkhouse and, beyond, a narrow stream glistened behind the corrals, handy for watering the ranch's horses.

'You've done really well, Johnny. Must've put a lot of sweat into this.'

'Lot of money, too,' Keyes said with pride. He still seemed a mite wary of Ronan. 'Had a room made up for you when I got word you were coming. Stay a few days, ride around: Chip'll show you over the place. See what you think. You want a job, I'll find you one.'

Allard remained blank-faced. Ronan pursed his lips and arched his eyebrows. 'Well, seems the "welcome" mat's out.'

'Hell, you're family, Gabe! Always have been, you know that.'

Ronan made an uncertain gesture. 'No, can't say that I did, Johnny.'

'What? Hell, man, we're *all* family! The whole damn wild-ass bunch of us!'

'I guess I used to think of it that way. When I was naïve. A word I learned the meaning of.' He watched their anxious faces. 'But I ain't been that for a long time. I realized a man's gotta do what he figures is best for himself. Like you fellers did. You, Johnny, and Chip, Milo, Shep and Ringo.'

'Now wait up! You could've give us up, but you didn't!' Keyes said sharply. 'I didn't see any sense in giving ourselves up when you were protecting us! I mean, we heard how they roughed you up and you

27

still never told 'em who was with you that night. If we'd've strode up and confessed, well, it would've been like you'd made those sacrifices for nothing. Least, that's how I looked at it.'

'And convinced the others without a helluva lot of trouble, I'd bet.'

Allard, waiting for a cue from Keyes, looked mighty uncomfortable. Keyes stubbed out his cheroot on the porch rail, looking at Ronan with steely eyes. 'You come back to square things with us?' *Straight from the shoulder.*

Ronan kept his face blank, let them sweat a little longer as the silence dragged on. Allard shifted from one foot to the other, clearing his throat. Keyes stood very still, tensed, waiting.

Then Ronan smiled crookedly. 'Relax. Sure, I figured out how things must've been for you fellers. I could've told the Judge what he wanted to know – pushed by Old Man Dawson, of course – but I didn't, so I did seven years hard-time. It was my choice.'

'Because we all took that stupid damn oath when we was in the army, Johnny!' Allard said with quick scorn. 'You know how it was, all young fellers, we'd been through the Wilderness, Bull Run, Little Round Top at Gettysburg and none of us had had a serious wound. So we figured we were a lucky group long as we stayed together and we took an oath that no matter what happened, we'd stick together, share the blame for any trouble and so on.'

'Judas priest, we were still full of sap and vinegar then!' Keyes said, half squinting at Ronan. 'You really remembered that oath and that's why you never gave us up? That's gospel, Gabe?'

Ronan held his gaze for a long moment. 'My old man taught me from an early age there were two things I *always* had to do in life if I wanted to be thought of as a decent human being: give my word and keep it, and take responsibilty for my actions. And that's what I did.'

'Now you're looking for some kind of compensation?' Keyes seemed ready to argue.

'Johnny, that's your notion. Chip's, too, I guess. Even Gant who barely knows me, figures I'll be after blood.' Ronan shook his head. 'It's done, over with. I can see by your faces, you don't believe me. Suit yourself. I'm not saying I don't hold some sort of grudge, but at the same time, I know I kept my mouth shut so whatever happened to me was my own fault. Now, settle for that. I'm going to.'

They gave him a lot of study before Johnny Keyes said, quietly, 'You really just want a job on my spread?'

'If there's one going; I don't want you to *make* a job for me. You got one, and it's to do with ranch work, I'll take it. Just remember, I ain't ridden a hoss in seven years till today and I'm already feeling kind of bow-legged. I ain't throwed a rope, branded a steer, fired a gun – don't count that on the train. That was just something that had to be done.'

Keyes suddenly smiled. 'Gabe, I've always said you're one of a kind and you've proved me right once again.' He opened the house door, stepped to one side and slid an arm about Ronan's shoulders. 'Come on inside and we'll toast your return in bonded Bourbon I ship in all the way from a brewery in Chicago.'

Ronan stopped suddenly and they snapped their heads around. Gabe smiled wryly. 'I ain't had anything stronger than watered-down coffee to drink in seven years, neither.'

Their laughter was too loud – with relief – and they went down the long shady passage and turned into the doorway of a living-room that had a ten-foot ceiling with two cut-glass chandeliers hanging from it. The walls were decorated with gilt-framed paintings and the furniture had that Eastern look to it: shipped in at great expense.

Gabe Ronan didn't know about the rest of them, but Johnny Keyes sure had plenty to lose.

If ever things should go wrong for him.

Ronan was sweating and aching by the time they topped out on what he remembered was called Fishtail Ridge at mid-morning. He mopped his face with a kerchief and Allard offered him the makings. When their cigarettes were burning, Gabe said, 'Johnny must own half the valley.'

Allard hesitated, then said quietly, 'So far.'

'Uh-*huh*, well he always was the ambitious one, why he was a lieutenant and the rest of us were just cannon-fodder.'

'You made sergeant, for a while.'

Ronan grinned ruefully. 'Stripes were just too damn heavy on my sleeve so I figured the best thing to do was get rid of 'em.'

'By takin' a town apart by yourself!'

'That was good corn-likker that Carolina cotton-picker gave us that night.' He hitched around in the saddle, wincing a little: his buttocks, unaccustomed to sitting leather, were throbbing. 'Where are the rest of the bunch, Chip? Didn't the Crocketts aim to prove up on land down there, along the river bottom?'

'Yeah. They did, too. Sold out to Johnny, though.'

There was something in the way that Allard said that last *sold out* that made Ronan's eyes pinch down some, and he took a long, thoughtful draw on his smoke.

'Milo Rafferty?'

'Hell, you know Milo.' He sounded evasive. 'He don't settle to anythin' for long. Drifts around the valley, works when he needs a few bucks. Even for the Dawsons.'

'And between times?'

Chip shrugged. 'We don't ask, Gabe. He's still got that hair-trigger temper. Meanest bastard in the County.'

The other was silent for the time it took to finish his cigarette. He stubbed it out against the saddle-horn. 'And how about the Crockett brothers now?'

He asked slowly and quietly and Allard looked at him sharply.

'Shep and Ringo, yeah! Well, they do the odd job for Johnny, got a cabin up in the Hotspurs, way back, and there's been a few complaints from other ranchers that they're in a good spot for allowing rustlers to drive stolen steers through the high pass behind their place. Dunno whether it's right or not, but they don't seem to do much to earn the money they spend in town.'

'Don't run cows themselves?'

'Rope a few mavericks and sell 'em to whoever wants 'em, including Johnny, but not enough to

31

support the way they live.'

'As I recall, they liked women.'

Allard smiled crookedly. 'Most times you'll find some female up there. You ain't asked about the Dawsons.'

Zachary Dawson was the biggest rancher hereabouts when Ronan had been sent off to jail. He'd been a tough, powerful man and it had been his youngest son, Owen, who had gotten killed in that stampede prank. He had demanded that Ronan be hanged but for some unknown reason there had been a change of heart a few days before the execution date and he had ended up in Purgatory Penitentiary on the rockpile instead.

'Well, what about him? From what you've showed me this morning, I can tell Dawson has lost a lot of his land to Johnny.'

'Yeah, the old man's dead now, died a few years back. Cutbank gave way under his hoss after heavy rain and he was drowned. Young Zac runs things now. Zac and Ellie.'

Allard was watching Ronan's face closely now. 'Well, Zac and me never did get along too well.'

'You work for Johnny and I'll guarantee you get along a whole lot worse now.'

'Feud?'

'S'pose you'd call it that. Johnny played smart with land deals, crowded the Dawsons so Zac had no choice but to give up some land and sell more to Johnny or go under. They call the ZeeDee just the "Zee" now, Zee bein' for "zero".'

'What!'

'Not quite, but Zachary's old spread has sure shrunk. Zac figured he was bein' smart here and there, makin' things more compact. Now that was fine in good seasons, but even Paradise Valley has drought and floods.'

'Noticed that dam up-river.'

'Bet you did. That belongs to Johnny and a bunch of other cattlemen. Formed a kind of syndicate. Members can get water for their stock no matter how dry it gets – other spreads can, too, but they have to pay – and at floodtime, when the dam's full they release the excess, which is sometimes too bad for some of the bottom-land settlers.'

Ronan noticed Allard moving a mite uncomfortably in his saddle. The man tended to look away rather than at him now. 'Johnny always did go hell-bent for what he wanted. Sounds to me like he's aiming to be king-pin of Paradise.'

'Right up there alongside God Almighty,' Chip said with a surprising amount of pride. Then he deliberately softened his tone. 'He's just a good businessman, Gabe.'

'By "good" you mean he's developed that old ruthless streak we all used to notice?'

'We-ell, They say there can't be any sentiment in business these days, Gabe. He changed after he got all that money from the railroad. Owns shares in it, too, I hear.'

'Not so popular in the valley, I guess.'

'No-oo, but he can be generous. He's helped out folk down on their luck. Othertimes I've seen him kick out a whole family with the man coughin' up his lungs because Johnny really needed their place.'

' "Wanted", more than needed by the sounds of it.' Ronan scratched his head under the hat, his hair sweat-damp. 'There've been more changes than I expected. Had it figured I'd be the only one to change much over the last seven years. Back to the Dawsons, Chip, how is Ellie? She married yet?'

Allard grinned. 'No, but I have to tell you, you won't stand much chance if you ride for the Key spread.'

'I never did have any kind of a chance. Too reckless and fiddlefooted for the likes of Ellie Dawson. She helps Zac run things, eh?'

'When Zac'll let her. You know what Old Zachary was like: a man's world, women stay in the kitchen, leave the chore of earnin' money to the man. Zac tries for most control, I reckon. Not sayin' she don't influence him – they was always pretty close for brother and sister, you recollect – but don't think she gets to make many major decisions. She works pretty damn hard, though, so I hear.'

'What's Johnny up to, Chip? Now don't look like that! You're his ramrod. You must have some idea. Is he gonna grab the whole damn valley eventually or what?'

'Johnny's plans are his own, Gabe. He don't confide in me. He gives the orders, I carry 'em out, like always. And he pays well. Damn well.'

Ronan nodded slowly, keeping his face carefully blank. 'OK.'

'He'll pay you well, too, Gabe. Know he feels bad about you havin' to do that prison time.'

'I dunno that he does. He's more worried about

what I might do now I'm back than what's already happened to me.'

Allard looked alarmed. 'Judas, don't get like that! Look, Gabe, you got a chance to make good here now. Let Johnny help you. We all owe you heaps, but we sort of look on Johnny as our leader, so go along with what he wants, OK?'

Ronan laughed shortly. 'You telling me that if I don't see eye-to-eye with Johnny Keyes, I'm gonna have the rest of the old bunch agin me?'

Allard had the grace to look embarrassed. But he didn't deny it.

They moved on and neither had much to say as they made their way into the Hotspurs, thickly timbered but with the vegetation hiding savagely gouged rocky canyons and dry washes a horse could tumble into beyond a screen of brush.

They saw Key-branded steers on the lower slopes and there were plenty of birdlife, some ground squirrels, chipmunks and even a brace of skunks in courting mood. Ronan remembered there had been timber wolves here, too, and figured that was why Johnny was keeping his steers closer to the ranch where his riders could keep an eye out for the predators.

There were a lot of Key riders, and he noticed they were all heavily armed. Each one they came across had a rifle either resting across his thighs or held cocked in his hands until they were identified to his satisfaction.

'Johnny hasn't forgotten his army days,' Ronan opined.

'The armed men? Lots of wolves still about, some two-legged. You can't own what Johnny owns, and do

35

it in such a short time, without makin' enemies, Gabe.'

Ronan had nothing to say to that.

Then Chip pointed across a dip between the hills, a little smoke rising above the dark green foliage high up.

'The Crocketts' place. Want to stop by and say "howdy"?'

Allard seemed a little reticent as he asked, as if hoping Gabe would say "no", but Ronan nodded. 'Why not? Been a long time.'

'It has.' Chip Allard spurred on ahead and Ronan heeled the sorrel after him, feeling a little uneasy about this but not knowing why.

Things were a hell of a lot different from what he had expected.

Maybe it was a hunch, because when they finally rode into the cluttered yard, the Crockett brothers were waiting for them.

Ringo, lean and wolfish, held his favourite weapon, a sawed-off Greener with barrels cut right down to the fore-end to ensure a wide spread of buckshot when he fired.

Shep, the hairy one with tobacco-juice stained beard, stood by the door of the ramshackle hut, a full-size Henry repeater rifle propped against the weathered logs beside him.

In his hand he held a cocked sixgun, stared hard at Ronan, then deliberately lifted the weapon, closed one eye and drew a bead on the visitor's head.

Before Ronan could react, Shep Crockett fired and Ronan spilled from the saddle.

CHAPTER 4

WELCOME BACK!

'Hey, Shep! Take it easy!' cried Allard, his horse prancing.

'You want one, too?' Shep asked with a wide grin that was almost lost in the bush of his beard. He lifted the smoking pistol. 'I can part your hair from here!'

'For Chris'sake!'

'How you doin' down there, Gabe?' Ringo asked, laughing, jerking the shotgun briefly. 'Shep ruin your new hat? Like your haircut, by the way!'

Stunned and with blood showing on his shirt over the wound in his side, Ronan got groggily to his feet, dusting himself off automatically. He glared at the grinning Crockett brothers and Ringo uncocked the shotgun and fixed it to the dog clip on his belt, which held reload shot-shells. Shep holstered his sixgun. Together they walked forward, right hands extended.

'Welcome back, Gabe!' Shep said.

'You always did know how to make a man feel

welcome, Shep,' Ronan said, smiling crookedly, reaching for Shep's hand.

Instead of shaking, he gripped the wrist and pulled Shep in hard against him, lifted a knee into the man's crotch. Shep gagged and his eyes widened even as his knees buckled. Ronan, still smiling into the man's pain-contorted face, yanked him close again, and head-butted him across the forehead, splitting the skin. Shep's eyes rolled up and Gabe let him fall to his knees, spinning towards Ringo.

Ringo was moving in fast, reaching for the sawed-off, but Gabe knew his tactics of old and spending seven years halfway to hell taught a man a lot of things. For one, how to move and, more importantly, when to move. The heavy gun was coming towards his head when Gabe twisted to one side, grabbed Ringo's left arm and pushed it up between the man's shoulders. Crockett grunted, tried to bring the shot-gun around. Ronan kicked it from his grip, shoved the arm a little higher and, as Ringo doubled over in an effort to ease the pain, brought a knee up into the man's face.

Allard stared, slack-jawed, as Ringo Crockett sprawled on his side in the dust, face ribboned with blood, his nose slammed hard-a-port, nostrils clogged with dark red. It had all happened in a matter of seconds.

'Jesus, Gabe! The hell're doin'! They never meant nothin'! You know Shep and Ringo were always practical jokers!'

'Lost my sense of humour in Purgatory, Chip.'

Shep was holding his hands clenched between his

legs, rolling about, groaning, looking up murderously at Ronan. Ringo was groggy, trying to sit up, spitting blood, more dripping from his chin. He glared at Gabe.

'You ruined my new shirt, goddamnit!'

Ronan laughed: he couldn't help it. Typical of a Crockett to worry about such things before he thought of his busted nose and loosened teeth. He stepped forward and helped Ringo to his feet and Crockett shook him off savagely.

'Get away from me, you goddamn jailbird!'

Ronan turned to Shep, gripped him under the arms and half lifted him, then dropped him back to the ground, hard. He did this three times, saying, 'That'll ease the pain, Shep, drop your balls back into their sheath.'

'Take more'n that to – ease – *your* goddamn pain when I get – up!' Shep allowed but didn't pull away when Ronan steadied him. He turned his reddened eyes to Gabe. 'You sonuvabitch! Guess that was your best hat I ruined, huh?'

Ronan grinned and this time he shook hands. 'If I still hadn't had a jail haircut you could've parted my hair, Shep.'

'Next time!' Shep promised unsmilingly.

'There won't be a next time,' Ronan said quite definitely and turned to Ringo who was swaying on his feet now. 'Howdy, Ringo. You want to shake or shoot?'

'I *want* to shoot, but I guess that'll keep a spell.' Ringo's words were thick and he spat to the left, then gripped hands with Ronan. 'Don't want you to think

I'm glad to see you, 'cause I ain't. You used to be able to take a joke, Gabe!'

'Lot of things've changed, Ringo, a whole lot. Can't afford to let anyone put anything over you in jail. Guess I just reacted. Seven years' habits are hard to shake.'

They knew he was apologizing, at the same time telling them 'no one messes with me these days.'

'Yeah, well, I guess that's right.' Ringo took Gabe by the upper arm, lowered his voice. 'Listen, seven years in the pen, you had to go without a lot of things, right?' He jerked his head towards the cabin door. 'Got us a little half-breed Comanche squaw inside. Barely sixteen but, man, does she know what it's all about. You're welcome to. . . ?'

Ronan smiled. 'Not right now, Ringo. Thanks anyway. I don't think Shep would like sharing her by the look of him.'

Shep *was* looking sour but he wiped his beard and limped across. 'You never used to hit a man below the belt, Gabe.'

'You heard me tell Ringo a lot of things've changed, Shep. Anyway, good to see you fellers.'

The Crocketts exchanged a glance that Ronan couldn't fathom and then he realized that, like Keyes and Allard, they were suspicious of his return, guilty consciences making them leery, figuring he would want to crack a few heads.

'You workin' for Johnny?' Shep suddenly asked.

'Not yet. But he's offered me a job.'

'Gonna take it?' Ringo sounded a little strained.

'Dunno, likely will. Just about flat broke.'

The Crocketts exchanged looks once more and Ringo frowned slightly, gave a small shake of his head. Ronan feigned indifference but inwardly he smiled: Ringo was telling Shep not to offer Gabe work in whatever they had doing way up here close to the high pass over the Hotspurs that would save a man driving a herd of rustled cows twenty miles. It could be a mighty lucrative deal, Gabe figured, and he had been kind of testing the Crocketts.

They didn't yet trust him, which came as no real surprise.

Ringo had the Indian girl make them some food – corn-patties and fried rabbit – which was barely palatable. She had big dark eyes, which she kept swivelling towards Gabe, and her buckskin dress was loose and slit high up one side. Shep grinned crookedly.

'We'd have to charge you, Gabe! She's costin' us plenty to keep here; her Old Man drives a hard bargain. Got to catch him a slew of ponies. Gonna get rid of her soon.'

Ronan nodded. 'He ought to take time to teach her how to cook.'

He saw no point in spending much time here. Shep and Ringo were as independent as ever and, if he wasn't mistaken, both men would never be far from a jug of corn-liquor or something alcoholic. He had no real beef with them but they did seem kind of peeved when he said he was leaving right after the meal.

'We want to know what you're gonna do,' Ringo said flatly.

'Dunno myself for sure,' Gabe answered easily.

41

'Just keep watching, you'll see soon enough.'

That didn't bring any smiles to the Crocketts' faces and Allard moved a little uneasily, too. Shep looked at the ramrod. 'Where you takin' him now?'

'Might see if Milo's around.'

'He ain't. Keeps to hisself lately and he ain't a happy man.' Ringo grinned. 'But let me know when he's gonna see Milo, you hear, Chip. I wouldn't want to miss that!'

'Me neither!' allowed Shep, smiling deep in his beard.

After they worked across the face of the mountain on a narrow, twisting trail, Ronan set his sorrel up alongside Allard's mount.

'What'd the Crocketts mean about my meeting with Milo?'

'Told you he don't care much for Johnny, nowadays. Nor anyone works for him. You show up and take a job on Key and he'll want to tear your head off.'

Ronan said nothing until they stopped to water the horses at a stream in a small canyon.

'We're getting over on to the old Dawson range here, ain't we?'

Allard glanced around, mildly surprised. 'Yeah, might've swung a mite wider than I aimed to, but this stream waters a lot of places. We should be OK. Genuine mistake.'

'What's that mean? 'Should be OK?'

Chip grimaced and scratched at his jaw. 'Well, I didn't spell it out proper earlier but there *is* a kind of feud goin' on between Key and ZeeDee.'

'Because of the way Johnny crowded out the Dawsons, bought 'em out and forced 'em on to a smaller spread that's maybe starting to pinch a little?'

Chip snapped his head up. 'You don't miss much!'

'Chip, I knew the Dawson spread almost as well as I knew that place we used as a camp in Drumroll Canyon. All I saw this morning were Key-branded cows on land that used to belong to Zachary Dawson and his kids.'

Allard nodded. 'Yeah, they lost a lot. but Johnny was just a smarter businessman, was all. Zachary was one of the old school, figured he didn't need to register claim on land that'd once been free range and he'd took and held it agin Injuns and everyone else who tried to take it from him. To him, a man made his camp and the land was his, far as a man could ride between sun-up and sundown. He refused to change when it became law for land to be filed on. That's where Johnny was smarter: while Zachary was still stewin' about it, rantin' agin the Gov'ment, Johnny went and filed on all that range.'

Ronan frowned. 'Johnny filed on land Zachary Dawson had been using for ten, fifteen years?'

'Using, yeah, but not legally his, strictly speakin'. It was all above board, what Johnny done.'

'Might've been legally but morally, well, I guess Johnny Keyes never was one to worry too much about that side of things.' He shook his head. 'It's a wonder it didn't develop into a shooting war.'

Chip dismounted and knelt to drink. Sitting back and wiping the back of a wrist across his wet mouth, he said, 'Was for a time: couple men got killed on both sides before Jake Gant stepped in and ended it.'

'That kind of range war doesn't "end" just because some badge-toter says so.'

'Gant's a hard man, Gabe. He . . .' Chip hesitated, then shrugged. Suddenly, wiping his face with a kerchief, he stiffened and looked sharply across the stream. 'Aw, damn!' he hissed.

Ronan, easing the girth on his sorrel, looked up and across his saddle. A small bunch of riders was coming across the shallow stream.

Four men and they all had rifles, the butts resting on their thighs, fingers through the trigger guards.

'That Zac Dawson in front?' Ronan asked quietly.

'That's him, bigger an' meaner than when you knew him. And in case you don't recognize him, the big feller alongside in the fringed buckskin-shirt and with the red bandanna tied round his head is . . .'

'Milo Rafferty!' cut in Ronan. 'What's he doing riding with the Dawson bunch?'

'Told you he didn't like Johnny nudging him off that bottom land. It's been a long time comin', but looks like he's finally done it and throwed in with ZeeDee.'

And just at that moment, the man with the red bandanna tied around his head instead of a hat, threw his rifle to his shoulder and fired. The bullet splashed water between Allard's boots at the edge of the stream. The ramrod jumped back as Milo Rafferty levered in another shell, swung the barrel to line up on Gabe Ronan.

'You're trespassin' on ZeeDee land!' Rafferty called.

'Can't blame you, I guess, Gabe, but that bastard Allard knows he oughtn't be here! Now both of you put your hands in the air and stand away from them mounts so we can see you plain. Zac has somethin' to say.'

Gabe Ronan watched Zac Dawson riding across and slowly climbed up into the saddle. Dawson hesitated.

'Don't you go anywhere, Ronan!'

'Didn't aim to.'

Dawson spurred his mount suddenly, teeth bared. He was a solidly built man and if Owen had lived, he might have taken on the same form. It could have been a young Zachary Dawson coming in fast and suddenly Ronan realized what the man was about to do. He wrenched the sorrel's head around, the long, sweat-dark body following, the horse giving a low whinny. Allard swore and jumped aside as Dawson swept in and past, rammed his claybank into Ronan's sorrel.

The horses squealed and floundered in the tangle as they hit and the sorrel started to go down. Gabe kicked his boots free of the stirrups and was diving out of the saddle when Dawson's heavy body came hurtling across. Zac took him high, long arms going around Gabe as they fell, struck the edge of the bank and rolled into the shallows.

They held on to each other as they splashed about, gravel digging into their bodies as they scuffled and floundered, trying to get to their feet. Both men heaved up almost at the same time, Gabe perhaps a mite faster. But he wasn't fast enough to dodge the hammering blow Zac slammed into the side of his neck. He went down, knocked away from the bank, and water closed over his head. A knee took him in the chest and forced him under. He choked as the river poured down his throat and his belly heaved as he closed his mouth tight, trying to find some air in his lungs.

Dawson's fists were pummelling, smashing down through the water, and surprisingly losing little of their force when they impacted. Gabe's need for air was desperate. His body twisted and writhed. His face broke free and he vomited the water he had swallowed. It hit Dawson in the face and the man reared back with a roaring curse. Ronan staggered halfway erect as Dawson savagely scooped water across his face, then, features contorted with his hate, charged back at Gabe.

Ronan wasn't quite upright but he managed to wrench aside so that Dawson's looping right swung past without touching him. The rancher staggered and dropped to hands and knees. Gabe lifted a boot and slammed the heel down between Zac's wide shoulders. Dawson grunted, the sound turning bubbly, as the force of the blow drove him under. He was quick to spin on to his back so that his face was uppermost and almost clear of the river. He flung a handful of gravel as Ronan kicked at his head, missed, and fell.

Zac came up like a leaping cougar, hands reaching for Gabe's throat. Ronan slapped them aside but the man's body crashed into him and they both went under again, churning the river shallows into mud

46

and foam. Knees rammed, elbows impacted hard, flesh split and blood made already slippery faces slimy and red-coated.

Zac Dawson seemed driven by a madness of hate that Ronan hadn't been prepared for but by now he knew this wasn't any normal fight: exchange a few blows and someone yell ' 'Nought' after a few teeth were loosened.

This was going to be a fight to the death if Zac had his way.

Gabe Ronan drove a straight left into the middle of the man's face as he lunged in. It connected with Zac's nose and mouth and stopped him in his tracks. Gabe shifted his attack to the midriff, hammered blow after blow into the rancher's ribs, doubling him over. He twisted fingers in the man's tangled wet hair, clogged now with river gravel, yanked his bloody face upwards and clubbed him between the eyes.

Dawson convulsed and fell face down in the water. Gabe, panting, dragging down deep, shuddering breaths, reached out to turn the man over so he wouldn't drown. His fingers barely touched Zac's shoulder when the man somehow corkscrewed upwards and rammed the top of his head under Gabe's jaw.

Ronan floundered, sat down in the shallows, the world appearing in swirling triple vision. The rancher closed, hands clawed, ready to throttle. Gabe had enough senses left to tuck down his chin, felt horny nails rip across his cheeks. He grabbed Zac's thick wrists – not as thick as his own rockpile-developed ones – twisted and, still holding on, spread

Dawson's arms wide. Zac wasn't expecting that and stumbled, scrabbling for a footing.

Ronan let go, set his own boots deep into a patch of underwater gravel, and hooked a savage blow deep into Dawson's ribs, well up into the arch. The man's eyes flew wide and his jaw dropped, his face suddenly taking on a bluish colour as he gagged and struggled to breathe.

Gabe Ronan floundered from the force he put behind the blow and watched Dawson's legs turn to jelly and the man sag down. He hit him alongside the jaw, well back under the left ear. Zac's head jerked, water spraying in a sunlit fan from his hair as he fell on his side, half in and half out of the river. Ronan dropped to his knees and then Chip Allard was helping him out on to the bank and saying wryly, 'Welcome back to Paradise, Gabe!'

'Still feels like I'm halfway to hell!'

CHAPTER 5

REDHEAD

Milo Rafferty came thrusting across the stream, his ugly face set in hard lines, a hand on his sixgun butt. He glanced at Allard and dismissed him as being no kind of a threat to him. Then he moved around past Dawson's fallen form and stood over Ronan who had now rolled on to his back. Gabe looked up at the towering Rafferty.

Milo curled a lip and drew back a boot but suddenly there was the whisper of metal against gun leather and Rafferty turned sharply, his own sixgun half-drawn.

He froze when he saw Allard covering him, Colt hammer cocked, shaking his head slowly. 'He's had enough, Milo. Leave him be.'

Rafferty looked uncertain, as if he would kick Gabe in the head anyway, then stepped back, lifting his big hands out to the side. 'I'll remember this, Chip!'

'Why don't you try rememberin' we all used to be pards, and how Gabe took the rap for us.'

'Shut up, you damn fool!' Rafferty gritted.

'You're the fool, ridin' for ZeeDee!'

Rafferty frowned, shifted the red bandanna on his head a little. 'Well, Johnny flim-flammed me. And I ain't about to forget it!'

'You ride for ZeeDee and you're a legitimate target for Key riders, Milo,' Allard pointed out. 'Anyway, why you so set agin Gabe?'

'Aw, you seen what he done to Zac! Hell, he's back to make us square away for what he done. I know that much!'

'You think you do. He took seven years of hell for the rest of us. He's a right to come back and see if we're grateful. Or not.'

Rafferty scowled. 'Be too damn late while you wait for him to show his hand! I tell you, I got no hankerin' to see the inside of Purgatory.'

Allard smiled thinly. 'Maybe Gabe'd send you all the way to hell, Milo. Look, give him a break. We're all leery, but knowin' the old Gabe, I reckon he'll do the right thing by us. He took that seven years' hard-time. You ask me, all he wants is a break now, chance to settle down, take up where he left off. Well, mebbe not that. He's older, tougher now, got more sense. But he says he aims to settle here. Johnny's offered him work if he wants it. I say we ought to give him a chance.'

Rafferty shook his head uncertainly. 'I dunno, it just don't feel right, somehow.'

'It ain't felt right for seven damn years!' Allard

snapped. 'We went on with our lives, Gabe suffered. We owe him plenty, Milo. *I* aim to give him a break. I can't speak for Johnny because he's, well, he's different to what he used to be. But he's told Gabe he can work for Key if he's a mind. And that's like offerin' a man your hand.'

'Sure! Where he can keep an eye on him! Johnny ain't no fool. He might seem to be givin' Gabe a break but he'll be watchin' close.'

'We all will, you blamed fool! But just watchin' is OK, see what he does.'

Rafferty grunted, swivelled his gaze to where Gabe was slowly sitting up, rubbing his swelling jaw, blood dripping from cuts on his face. 'Howdy, Milo. Why don't you do what Chip says? Just wait and see.'

Rafferty frowned. He knew by Gabe's tone that the man was toying with him but such was his uncertain mood that he didn't want to show any softening of his attitude.

'I'll be watchin', all right, damn close!'

Then he knelt beside the stirring Dawson, took the man's hat from where it had fallen, dipped it in the stream and poured it over the rancher's head. Zac took a few minutes to come round and by that time, the two cowboys had crossed the stream and were sitting their mounts, still holding their rifles, awaiting orders. Dawson groaned as he allowed Rafferty to help him to his feet. He tried to glare at Ronan but his eyes were too swollen and reddened to have much effect.

'You bastard! You oughta be dead, 'stead of standin' there lookin' at me like you want to kill me.'

51

'Not particularly, Zac, but I won't turn my back on you for a spell.'

Dawson swore. 'Get off my land, damn you! You lousy murderer!'

Ronan thought he was referring to Owen's death in the stampede, but then Zac added, 'Big Zachary'd still be alive today if it weren't for you!'

Gabe blinked. 'How you figure that? I been in jail for the past seven years! He died five years back, they tell me.'

'Yeah! Broken-hearted over Owen, who was always his favourite, him bein' the last born to Ma before she died. Zachary doted on that boy, spoiled him rotten, and the life drained outta him after Owen was killed by you!'

Ronan frowned. 'You saying Zachary killed himself? That his drowning was his own doing?'

'It was *your* doin'! *You* killed him no matter where you were at the time! He pined for Owen so bad that—' Zac's voice broke and he paused, took a deep breath, scarred hands clenching at his sides. 'He just couldn't stand it any more! He'd often said that he figured drownin' would be as good a way as any to go, give yourself up to the water, ease yourself into death!'

'Zac, that cutbank gave way, softened by the flood rains,' Allard said in a surprisingly gentle voice. 'Jake Gant investigated and he's no fool.'

'He didn't know Pa like I knew him! And you stay outta this, Chip. This is between him and me!'

He managed to get some hate and passion into his voice and look this time. Ronan didn't flinch.

'I guess there's no reasoning with you, Zac,' he said quietly. 'You know damn well you can't blame me for Zachary's death.'

'I damn well can! And I will! You're gonna be mighty sorry you come back to this valley, Ronan! *Mighty* sorry! Now get off my land before I have my men shoot you!'

There was no point in arguing. Milo Rafferty looked confused but he mounted again and aligned himself with Zac and his cowboys. Gabe mounted stiffly and he and Chip rode slowly away.

'Never seen Zac that crazy before,' Chip murmured.

'He's kind of got his thinking all twisted,' Gabe admitted. 'Guess he's got a lot on his mind what with losing so much land to Johnny Keyes, and his father and kid brother both dead. Ellie feel the same way as Zac?'

Allard looked sharply at Ronan: the man was trying to make his enquiry casual, but Allard sensed the answer was important to Gabe.

'Don't see much of her. I told you, she does the ranch books, keeps tally, orders supplies, once even handled a couple of meat agents that didn't want to come into the valley, so she met 'em at a railhead with a sample bunch of cattle. Riled Zac all to hell, she got such a good price.'

Ronan nodded, face expressionless. 'She always tried to involve herself in the running of the ranch as I recollect. Not that old Zachary approved. S'pose she thinks the way Zac does. About me, I mean.'

'Told you I dunno. Wouldn't worry about it. She

don't leave the ranch often. You ain't likely to run into her.'

When he was sure they had crossed the ZeeDee-Key line, Chip made a stop, heated some water and doctored some of Gabe's cuts and bruises. Gabe was grateful. He had had plenty of fights in prison – a man *had* to fight or get ground down in there – but this one was almost as bad as he could remember. Dawson had been like a madman, inflicting damage recklessly, uncaring about his own hurts, wanting only to kill him, beat him to death.

That had happened in prison a few times, but Zac seemed to be driven by a madness that had left Gabe mighty sore. And some stitches in his wound had broken, the gaping lips torn and bleeding copiously now.

'Wad a cloth and ram it down into the wound, then bind it in tight as you can,' he instructed Allard who seemed dubious.

'You need a sawbones, Gabe. We better get on into town. We can cut across by Fishtail Ridge from here, save several miles.'

'Just patch me up, Chip. No, don't argue! Do what I say. I'll be all right.'

'You'll be sick and sorry is what you'll be, but OK. I'll just patch you up.'

After it was done, Gabe moved about stiffly but felt better with his side strapped up and the wound plugged. Not that he wasn't suffering but, as he had said, he'd had worse in prison – not much mind! – and had to get over it without more than token help from the first-aid room. The prison doctor was more often drunk than sober enough to tend prisoners' wounds.

'We best be gettin' back to the ranch house, I guess,' said Allard, glancing up at the sun in the sky. 'You've seen most of the place now, not close-up, but you can tell how big it is from those high places we stopped.'

'Yeah, almost half the valley. You go on back, Chip, I want to ride over to that quarter-section I'd been thinking to prove up on before all the trouble.'

'That's part of Key now, Gabe.' Allard spoke tightly, reticent about pointing out this fact.

'Yeah, I know. Saw it in the distance from one of those peaks where we stopped. Just want a closer look at it. As I recollect it was in a fold of the hills, and I'd had a notion of building a cabin on the rise, looking across the valley and the river, reminded me of the place where I grew up.'

'We've got a lineshack up there, Gabe,' Allard said, still speaking slowly, sensing there just might be more to this than what Gabe was saying. 'Johnny's got plans for that later, throwin' a small dam across between the slopes just to water those flats that run out towards the big pass.'

Gabe frowned. 'Johnny's got all that land, too?'

Allard smiled. 'Told you, he aims to own *all* of the valley some day. He's got big plans.'

Ronan said nothing, went to his horse and tightened the cinchstrap, then, about to put a boot into the stirrup, turned to Chip. 'Haven't worn a gun in seven years, Chip, but, well, I'd feel better packing iron after what's happened. Lend me your Colt? Or your rifle, one or t'other, don't matter which.'

Allard hesitated, then nodded, unbuckled his gunbelt and handed it to Ronan. He watched the man put it on easily, reach for the tie thong at the holster base and knot it around his thigh. He settled the rig to his liking, pulled the Colt out and spun the cylinder. Chip grinned.

'Doin' what comes naturally, huh? Seven years since you wore a gun and first thing you do is check the loads!'

Ronan smiled. 'Some things you never forget, Chip. Thanks for the gun. Be back at the spread by sundown.'

'I can come with you.'

'No, it's OK, wouldn't mind some time alone. That's one of the worst things being penned up. Unless you get solitary, you never have a moment when you're alone, pushed and beat and shoved with men crushing against you all the time.'

Allard was sober now. 'Sure, Gabe, sure. See you come sundown.'

Chip watched Ronan ride away towards the hogback that hid the lineshack and Gabe's old quarter-section from view. The man sat that horse like he was part of it, the same way that gun rig seemed to grow right out of his lean body.

Like it belonged there.

He came into the small valley from the low end, having skirted the brush belt that faded eventually into the plains. Looking up at the ridge, he could see how it would be comparatively simple to throw up a log wall between the folds, trapping flood water, using it by means of headgates and irrigation channels to bring on pasture that would support hundreds of head of cattle, instead of allowing the water just to drain away and erode the land as it did now.

Yeah, Johnny Keyes had his head screwed on the right way, all right. *Big dam for the valley, small one for new pasture. And he would control the water.* Ronan hadn't realized just how ambitious the rancher really was.

That railroad money for land in his name hadn't hurt any, he guessed: it had enabled Johnny to build up his plans, maybe extend them. *Good luck to him: he'd been smart enough to look out for himself while the rest of the bunch had been raising hell – he deserved to make a success of things.*

And, knowing Keyes, Gabe reckoned he would do just that, at whatever cost. Because Johnny Keyes had a cold ruthless streak that was usually found in ambitious men who figured themselves as empire-builders.

Then he heard the gunfire as he rode out of a heavy stand of timber.

Gabe reined down sharply, soothing the startled sorrel, leaning over it and stroking one side of its neck as he listened and looked up-slope.

It was coming from up there, about where the line-shack would be, he figured. Desultory shooting. Maybe just someone popping old bottles, sighting-in a rifle, a Henry he figured by the flat, short sound of the shots.

Then there came the more whiplashing sound of two fast shots from a Winchester.

Two shooters. The echoes rolled around the slopes but he figured one was coming from the ridge on his right, the other, the Henry sound, from higher up. *Lineshack. Someone holed up in the lineshack, being pot-shotted by someone else on the ridge.*

He wished he had borrowed Chip Allard's rifle instead of the sixgun, realizing with something of a shock, that he was going to go up there and buy into the fight if necessary. And if that's what all the shooting was about.

He didn't stop to reason it out, put his heels to the sorrel's flanks and set it up the slope, keeping to the timber where he could. There wasn't much shooting going on now, so maybe he had it all wrong, might just be two different men sighting-in their guns. *Maybe.*

Then the Henry rapped in a short, sharp barrage of shots – five at least, possibly six – and the Winchester answered with just one. He swerved the sorrel, dismounted stiffly, knifing pain from his wound catching his breath.

Colt in hand, unable to crouch properly because of the wound, he made his way through the timber, smelling woodsmoke, likely from the stove in the lineshack. It took him more time than he had expected to work his way on to the ridge. Sweating, trying to control his heavy breathing and feeling slightly dizzy, he wiped a hand across his swollen, blackened eyes, trying to see up there. *Yeah!* He saw a man's trouser-clad legs protruding from a small group of rocks. The faded blue of a shirt showed as the man moved, awkwardly it seemed to Ronan, fumbling at the loading gate of his Winchester.

He distinctly heard a groan and figured whoever was up there was wounded. Then the rifle crashed but it clattered as it fell from the grip of the shooter. By then, Ronan had worked up behind the man and he glimpsed the lineshack down below, some of the roof shingles shot away, the door splintered from several bullets. Looked like the siege had been going on for some time.

The man below and before him groaned again, rolling slowly on to one side. Gabe was surprised to see it was Sheriff Jake Gant. And there was a lot of blood on the sheriff's blue shirt around waist level, more soaking into the earth beneath the lawman's body.

Gant tensed and jumped, tried to spin around as Ronan crawled up alongside him. 'How bad're you hit?'

Gant had tried to bring the rifle around but stopped now, his face grey and pain-drawn, as he recognized Gabe.

'Damn near shot you!'

'You were a long ways from doing that. Your wound?'

Gant eased back and let Gabe see the bullet-torn furrow running from up on his ribs down into the pad of flesh and muscle just above the hip. The flesh was torn badly and Gant had tried to pack a bandanna over it to stop the bleeding, but without much success.

'Feel kind of light-headed. Floatin' away . . .'

'I'll have to rip up your shirt to make a bandage.'

'OK, but keep your head down or you'll get it shot off.'

Working, ripping the blue cloth, Gabe asked, 'Who is it?'

'Red Abbott.'

Ronan stopped, holding the bloody shirt. 'The one you figured was in on the train robbery? I winged him.'

Gant nodded. 'Was his trail of blood that led me up here. Knew he and his pards hung out here just past the edge of the plains – easier for a quick getaway, see? – but forgot about the line camp. They been holed up here, I reckon.'

He almost passed out now as Ronan moved him and wrapped the shirt over the wound, knotting it tightly. Two shots came from the Henry, the lead whining off the rocks that screened the lawman and Gabe.

'He's not a bad shot,' Ronan opined.

'Figure he's about out of ammo, for the rifle, anyway. He ain't been shootin' off his Colt. Might not even have one now, but I wouldn't bet on it.'

'OK that's about as good as I can do for your wound. How much rifle ammo you got?'

'Whatever's in the magazine, four shells, I think. Might only be three or possibly only two.'

Gabe swore. He worked the lever fast and three cartridges were ejected. He thumbed them home, eased the sixgun in Allard's holster.

'You're goin' down after him?'

'Isn't that what you want me to do?'

Gant managed a faint smile. 'It's what I figured you'd do. Had it in mind myself before he winged me, the sonuver. Guess you dunno this place, but there's a thick brushline to the right.' He tried to point but lifting the arm hurt his wound and he cursed instead. 'You can get within five yards of the door. No door in the back and only that one shuttered window to the left of the door. But he's mean and he's a good shot. You'll need to move fast.'

Gabe nodded: just what he felt like doing after the fight with Zac Dawson and his own wound bursting open!

'By the way, you win that fight?' Gant asked as he made to move away.

Ronan didn't answer, crawled on his belly out of the rocks, dropping over a small ledge and sliding down to the brushline Gant had mentioned. He still couldn't crouch without pain, and moved lower down the slope, away from the lineshack.

When he figured he was level with it, he turned left and made his way in. The bushes stirred with his passage and there was a shot from the lineshack. He ducked, hearing the lead rustle through the brush, twigs and leaves dropping around him. Through a gap, he could see the front of the shack now and the splintered door seemed to be open a little wider than previously.

He couldn't hesitate now that Abbott had his position so he leapt up as fast as he could, plunged through the brush, feeling the tug at his clothing, the searing scrape of twigs across his wounded area.

Teeth bared, he ran in, boots pounding, saw too late that Red Abbott was lying prone just inside the doorway. The Henry banged and Gabe felt the tug of the slug going through the slack of his shirt and then he had the Winchester's butt braced into his hip, working lever and trigger.

The three shots roared out and he kept working twice more before he realized it, dropped the rifle, snatched at his Colt and shoulder-rolled across the doorway. He glimpsed Abbott and the man had a sixgun in his hand now, fired even as Gabe put two shots through the doorway. Dust choking him as he rolled, the jarring pain from his wound unnoticed for the present, he skidded around and beaded the redhead once more.

'Don't!' croaked Abbott, lifting the hand with his sixgun, dangling it by the trigger guard around one finger. 'I – I'm bad – hit!'

Ronan didn't move, aware he was in the open here. 'If I shoot it'll go right through the middle of your face, Red!'

'Don't – I – give up!'

'Can you stand?'

'Don't think so . . .'

'Then crawl out where I can see you! I'm not coming in there!'

'I – I'm alone. You finished – my pards on the – train.'

'Too bad I didn't finish you, too. You were there to stop me coming back to the valley.'

Silence, except for a kind of bubbly breathing from Red Abbott.

'Who wanted me dead, Red? Longer you take to answer, longer it'll be before I can get you to a sawbones.'

'Aw, *shoot*! I think I'm dyin'! You gotta – help me!'

'Help yourself. Tell me who sent you to kill me on that train and you're on your way to a sawbones.'

'All right – all – right! But you gotta – protect me.'

'Judas priest! *Who the hell was it?*'

Red lifted to one elbow, blood trickling from one corner of his mouth as he opened it to speak.

Then a rifle crashed from up on the ridge and Abbott's body spun back into the dimness of the line-shack and Ronan clearly heard the man's death rattle as he flopped over on to his back, his face destroyed by the bullet.

Gabe Ronan whirled on to his own back, savagely angry as he brought the sixgun around.

A man waved to him from the ridge.

'Gant?'

Gabe frowned, squinting against the sun.

'Chip, Gabe. Saw the gun in his hand and you moved just enough to let me get a clear shot. I get him?'

Ronan slumped and holstered the Colt, clambering to his feet. 'Yeah, you got him, Chip. Come on down.'

CHAPTER 6

NIGHT LIGHTS

Coming in via the trail out from the Key spread, Providence looked a much larger town than it actually was. There were more lights than Ronan expected, but then he hadn't seen nightlights stronger than a turned-down lantern or a candle-stub for seven years.

But if the town had impressed him with its progress during the day when Gant had first brought him in, this night-glimpse of Providence almost amazed him.

'Looks like one of the wide-open towns we used to raise hell in on the early cattle drives,' he allowed. 'Wichita, Dodge, even Ellsworth, and that town had plenty of lights.'

'Yeah, she's pretty well supplied with saloons and a few cat houses,' Allard told him, stifling a yawn: it had been a long, long day and it wasn't over yet.

They were sitting in the driving seat of a buck-

64

board, Allard handling the reins, Ronan beside him, holding the new bandages tightly over his wound, which refused to stop bleeding. Their horses were tied to the tailgate, but in the bed of the wagon Jake Gant lay supine, occasionally moaning, his side thick with bandages. His wound, too, was still bleeding and this had prompted Johnny Keyes at his ranch when the wounded men had been brought in by Chip Allard to say what they needed was expert medical attention. And that meant a trip to town to the doctor.

'Jake looks like the doc'll keep him in the infirmary for a spell,' the rancher opined, looking down at the sheriff's pale, gaunt face. 'But Gabe'll be OK if he gets his wound stitched again. He can stay in my room at the hotel.'

Ronan had looked up sharply as Keyes' grey-haired housekeeper bathed away the dirt and dried blood from his gaping wound. 'You keep a room in town?'

Johnny smiled as he lit another of his cheroots. 'Sure, only one decent hotel, the Gateway, and only one decent set of rooms so I keep 'em on permanent standby for when I ride into town and stay overnight.'

Ronan arched his eyebrows. 'Living high on the hog, Johnny!'

Keyes shrugged indifferently. 'What I've always aimed for. The only way to live. Anyway, you stay there long as it takes for you to heal, Gabe. Come on back here when you're ready to go to work. There'll be a job for you.'

Ronan thanked him, thinking that Keyes seemed to have more surprises waiting every time they met.

He had organized the housekeeper to go to work on Gant as soon as Allard had brought him in with Gabe coming in a quarter mile behind. Keyes saw that Gant needed attention first and while the housekeeper worked over him questioned Chip, who told him succinctly about the shootout at the line camp.

'Thought Gabe didn't see the sixgun in Red Abbott's hand from where he was set up. Was about to yell when he moved just enough for me to draw bead on Red so I nailed him – dead centre.'

Keyes stared back at his ramrod. 'Killed him? You always did shoot to kill, even on prisoner-catchin' raids.'

'He's dead *and* buried, Johnny, out back of the shack.' Chip Allard spoke easily, indifferently.

Gabe came limping up the steps then, after leaving his horse with trailing reins to be looked after by one of the ranch hands. Johnny hurried to the steps and took his arm, helping him into a chair.

'Mrs Denny'll be with you pretty soon, Gabe, working over the sheriff right now. Chip was telling me you had a close call with Red Abbott.'

Ronan glanced at Chip. 'I thought you didn't see the sixgun in his hand, Gabe. Figured I'd best shoot quick.'

'It was empty. He was just about to tell me who paid him and his pards to rob that train – as a cover for killing me.'

Keyes frowned, leaned forward swiftly in his own cane chair. 'A cover to kill *you*? What the hell for,

Gabe? You make some bad enemies in that prison?'

Ronan smiled faintly. 'Made some somewhere. No, it wasn't anyone I tangled with in jail, Johnny.'

'Well, you can't be sure, can you?' Keyes said, adding quickly. 'I mean, Red didn't tell you anything, did he?'

Gabe shook his head. 'No, Chip was too good a shot.'

'Well, it don't matter, does it? You're here now and we'll make sure no one tries to kill you, if anyone does have such a notion.'

Ronan got the message: they doubted him but he wasn't about to try to justify his hunch, so merely nodded. Then, as Keyes was relaxing and Chip was lighting a cigarette, he said, 'Red had been living in that shack for quite a while, signs of two or three of 'em, matter of fact.'

Keyes frowned. 'Red Abbott and his pards living in *my* line camp?' He glared at Allard. 'You're s'posed to check all the line camps regularly, Chip! What the hell?'

Allard looked worried. 'The men know they gotta do it, Johnny. Certain men do certain areas. Check the line camps at least once every two weeks, every week in winter when we're more likely to get squatters and lose the stores. I'll kick a few butts over this 'cause Gabe's right: there was plenty of sign to show two, three men had been makin' themselves at home there.'

'Sons of bitches!' Keyes' face was angry. 'Goddammnit, Chip, I'm holding you responsible! You send men to check every line camp we've got in the morning! They find anyone there, they kick 'em out, kick their asses first or bust their heads. If they still fuss, shoot 'em!'

'That's going back to the bad old days, ain't it, Johnny?' Gabe asked quietly, Keyes' cold eyes swivelling towards him.

'It's how I run things, Gabe! How I *want* 'em run. I make the rules out here in the valley and I still believe in hanging rustlers on the spot. Jake Gant'll savvy that sooner or later.'

Which meant that the sheriff didn't necessarily go along with Johnny Keyes' rules in Paradise Valley. There could be more conflict here than Gabe was seeing right now.

Kind old Mrs Denny doctored his wound and agreed with Keyes that it should be re-stitched. So they drove on into Providence and arrived at the doctor's place, followed by a small group of rubbernecking townsfolk, a few drunks shouting questions.

'The sheriff can stay here a day or two,' Doctor Dundee told Allard. He was a weary-looking man in his fifties, not very large, but there was a strength about his jaw that told Ronan here was a man dedicated to his profession, likely wore himself out visiting sick folk all over the valley or wherever he got a call from. 'As for Mr Ronan, here, well, you've got the constitution of a mountain lion, sir: anyone who walks around with that tangle of scars like you have on your back, *has* to be tough. I think you'd be wise, though, to spend the night right here.'

'Johnny Keyes says he can have his private room at

the Gateway, Doc,' spoke up Allard and the medico pursed his lips.

'As long as it's alone. You get my meaning, Mr Ronan?'

'I get it, Doc. All I want to do is sleep round the clock.'

The doctor turned to Allard and shook a finger at him. 'If that's what he wants to do, you see that it happens, Chip. Tell them at the hotel Mr Ronan is not to be disturbed, and allowed to wake in his own good time.'

'Consider it done, Doc. Er, sheriff gonna be OK?'

Dundee nodded wearily, gathering his instruments. 'Another one who no doubt eats his meat raw.'

Chuckling, Allard and Ronan left and twenty minutes later, Gabe was asleep in the big, soft bed in Johnny's private rooms at the Gateway Hotel.

He slept well enough but there had been disturbing dreams, strange, violent ones, mixed up with the prison and the years of war. He saw a lot of familiar faces belonging to dead men.

But he had a good appetite for breakfast and was surprised to find it was after ten o'clock as he started on his third cup of coffee. Allard had to get back to the ranch and left some money with Gabe to buy some spare clothing.

And ammunition for the sixgun and rifle he had taken as spoils of war from the lineshack. He sent out for some gun oil and cleaning kits, a set of screwdrivers and pliers. Then he spread newspapers over the polished oval table and disassembled the rifle first, afterwards the Colt. Both weapons had been neglected, needed not only old powder residue cleaned from where it clogged vents and springs and action slides, but also the firing mechanisms required adjustment.

He was pleased to find that he hadn't forgotten how to service and tune his firearms. He loaded both weapons and felt an urge to go try them out some-where. His wound was sore but nothing he couldn't handle, and Chip had said he would leave his sorrel at the livery for him.

So he ate lunch at the hotel and left there about mid-afternoon, wearing the Colt tied down to his right thigh, carrying the oil-sheened Winchester as he made his way to the livery stables. He had to pass the infirmary and called in to see how the sheriff was doing.

'You won't find him here if that tells you anything!' growled Doc Dundee. 'Man's crazy. Was up before daylight, yelling for his clothes and didn't let up until he had them. I dare say you'll find him in the law office, if he isn't out chasing down some outlaw!' He shook his head again. 'Damn fool. Now don't you go straining that wound of yours, either! It won't take any more stitches and you could bleed to death. Or get an infection that'll kill you.'

'Promise I'll be careful Doc,' Ronan said, smiling, as he waved and continued on.

He was going to call in and see Gant, then thought better of it, swung back to cross the street to the livery.

She must have seen him coming and waited in the

shadows of the first stall as he entered and called to the hostler raking straw at the far end of the aisle: 'I'm Gabe Ronan. Chip Allard left a horse for me here last night. Big sorrel with the Key brand.'

The man gestured with the rake handle to a stall about halfway along. Gabe waved thanks and started towards the stall. He stopped dead when he felt the gun muzzle ram roughly against his spine and a voice full of hostility snapped, 'Get your hands up! Now!'

He lifted his hands slowly, still holding the rifle.

'Drop that gun!'

'If it's all the same to you, ma'am, I'll just set it down gently on the ground at my feet. I just spent a couple hours cleaning and adjusting it and don't want to jar it.'

'Then do it! And it had better be gently or I'll shoot! Don't you think I won't!'

'I believe you, ma'am,' Ronan said, grunting a little as he stooped to lay the Winchester on the straw-littered ground beside his right foot. As he straightened, grunting again, he turned slowly and faced his captor, his hands raised.

She'd changed little in seven years. Oh, sure, a few more lines, worry or weather, on that oval face with the clear skin. But the eyes were as feisty as ever, narrowed now so they looked jet black but he knew they were hazel-coloured in reality. She had pushed back her hat to hang by the rawhide thong, revealing the masses of brown, wavy hair and the sight of it made his palms tingle, but it had been a long, long time since he had caressed those silken tresses.She still only reached his shoulder, her body small and

71

giving the impression of firmness even under the loose-fitting cream blouse and denim work trousers. Her boots, as he remembered, were scuffed and dirt-caked from ranch work.

'See you still like to work the spread, Ellie.'

'When Zac lets me, and what there is of it nowa-days!' she retorted, the cupid's-bow lips compressing. 'Thanks to your friend Keyes and his underhand methods!'

'I heard he done everything legal, that Zachary was just too stubborn to put things to rights with the Lands Department. He . . .'

He wasn't prepared for her reaction. She took a quick step forward and slapped him with her free hand, the sixgun in her other hand ramming him in the belly. He grunted and sagged a little, stepping back, rubbing his mid-section gingerly.

'He took advantage of a sick old man! And don't *you* bad-mouth my father! It's because of you that he's dead. Just as you're to blame for Owen's death! You damn murderer! When Zac told me he'd fought with you I cursed him for not drowning you in the river when he had the chance.'

'Well, he may've had the chance and tried, but he wasn't good enough.' Ronan said it deliberately to make her mad and, as he hoped, she lunged at him again.

He grabbed the hand with the gun, twisted the weapon free, hunched a shoulder to take her blow and then spun her around gasping as he pushed her arm up between her shoulder blades.

'Hey!' called the hostler from the end of the aisle

but he made no move to approach.

'Go about your chores, friend,' Gabe called without looking at him. The girl struggled until she realized the more she did so, the more her arm hurt. 'Goddamn you, Gabe Ronan!'

'Someone did, Ellie. Now take it easy. I don't want to hurt you.'

'Hurt me all you like! It won't change anything! We'll kill you sometime, you murdering son of a bitch!'

Gabe tut-tutted. 'That's new, you cussin'. But maybe you already tried to have me killed, huh? Red Abbott and his pards on the train? You and your brother put them up to it?'

She peered at him over her shoulder, hair hiding half of her face. But he saw her puzzlement was genuine.

'We've never had anything to do with Red Abbott and his friends! They're cheap, drunken outlaws and . . .'

'They're dead. All three.'

She drew down a deep breath. 'Ye-es, I did hear about you killing the two on the train, but Red?'

'Last night, Key line camp in the Hotspurs.'

'Ah. Our horse-wrangler was looking for mustangs and he said he thought he heard shooting in the hills late yesterday.' She tossed her hair. 'So it was you, back a day and a half, and with three dead men at your feet! I might've expected as much!'

Ronan looked at her and she must have felt disconcerted for she stammered when she spoke. 'What? Why're you looking at me like that? You seem

73

almost surprised.'

'S'pose I am a mite. Never thought we'd be friends again, Ellie, but, well, I didn't expect you like this.'

She scoffed. 'After you killing my kid brother and my father?'

He shook her, surprising her so that she blinked. 'That's hogwash and you know it. Owen, well, I guess it was partly my fault he got caught up in that stampede.'

'You admitted as much! They put you in jail for it!'

'And I did seven years on that account. Your father died while I was in prison, Ellie. Don't tell me you go along with Zac's stupid notion that I caused your father to commit suicide.'

'Why not? It could be true.'

'Hogwash again. I'm not gonna even try to explain. You know damn well deep down it was an accident just as Jake Gant found when he investigated. If it *was* suicide, there's no one to confirm that, and I still don't admit responsibility. No! Just shut up! You've had your say and I reckon I've said all I'm going to, as well.'

He thrust her from him but rammed her sixgun into his belt and scooped up his rifle. She stood there, face flushed, eyes blazing, small fists bunched.

'Don't you dare speak to me like that!'

'Go home, Ellie, and leave me be. I came back to settle down. Seems a lot of folk won't believe that. Well, I don't give a damn what anyone believes, and that includes you. I may move on, but these past seven years I've had me a bellyful of being pushed around and told to do this or that. So whatever happens, *I'll* decide for myself. Anyone doesn't like it, then they can come to me and tell me and see what it gets them.'

'What'll you do? Kill them?'

'If I think they need killing.'

Her lips curled, tears welling in her eyes despite her resolve to stay dry-eyed. 'And I suppose that would include me, too!'

He gave her a cold look, shook his head kind of sadly, then walked on down to the stall to where his sorrel waited.

By the time he had it saddled, Ellie Dawson had gone.

And he neither knew nor cared where.

CHAPTER 7

TARGET PRACTICE

The place he had in mind for trying out his guns was no longer suitable.

Flood rains and new vegetation had changed the dry gulch over the years so that it was almost choked with greenery and the earthen wall he had figured would make a good backstop for the bullets had eroded and collapsed.

He sat there at the entrance, looking at it while thinking of some other place he could recall that would be suitable. It came to him abruptly and he turned the sorrel in the same moment and caught a flash of something on the ridge above, maybe a piece of clothing, disappearing swiftly amongst the boulders up there.

He didn't want an audience.

Not that he was shy in any way but he just didn't care to have someone monitoring his shooting, or general movements for that matter. Making a sudden decision, he rammed his heels into the sorrel and lifted the reins with a muted yell of encouragement: '*Eeeh-yaaa*!'

The horse lunged with a small snort of protest and he half stood in the stirrups, moving the reins easily this way and that as the well-trained range horse weaved its way through the trees. Gabe didn't figure he would be able to jump whoever it was up there, but he reckoned they would light out and leave him be. He might even catch a glimpse of the spy.

Maybe it was only because of the hard years in prison where a man had to be suspicious of everyone twenty-four hours a day, but he wasn't really relaxed back here in Paradise Valley.

His hunch or sixth sense or whatever you wanted to call it hadn't been blunted, he was sure. It had worked well enough in Purgatory, literally saved his neck on a couple of occasions. So he wasn't about to dismiss the feeling now that someone was keeping tabs on his movements.

But when he reached the ridge top, he was not surprised to find it deserted. He didn't even have to dismount to see the broken twigs and hoof-scarred patches where the spy had vacated his vantage point in a hurry.

Gabe found some horse hair caught on one broken twig, but there wasn't enough to be sure if it was brown or claybank, roan or chestnut. Crashing the sorrel through brush that brought him out to a point where he could look down the far slope gained him little.

There was a thin haze of yellow dust drifting but

no sign of a rider.

Gabe said the hell with it: he didn't aim to waste time looking. If whoever it had been was serious they would try to track him again, and he would be alert.

After riding aimlessly, looking for a suitable place to sight in and fine-tune his weapons, Gabe remembered there was a draw that used to branch off a small canyon he thought had been called Stillwater, because it was close to a quiet bend of the river that kept a small waterhole permanently filled in the sandstone trough in the canyon floor.

The draw ran off almost directly above that mirror-like pool. He smiled faintly as he remembered he and Ellie Dawson had had a couple of picnics there, long ago now.

Yes, it was as he recalled it, shaped like an arrow-head, high earthen walls meeting in a rough point that would absorb the bullets. A small clump of boulders at the canyon end, interspersed with patches of sand and little vegetation would make a good spot to shoot from. He paced it out and it was just over a hundred yards: a fine distance for sighting-in a rifle. It made it easy to allow for shorter or longer distances, especially with the flip-up Vernier scale sight. It was a good quality rifle and he figured Red Abbott or his pards had likely stolen it.

The crash of the Winchester hurt his ears because the draw was small and confined, but it would also hold in the sound of gunfire, keep it from rolling too far by the time it passed down the canyon.

He started out with twigs placed in a row in the sand, adjusted his barrel sights until he could split each one in two with a single shot, working down a line fast. His father had taught him to shoot that way.

'If Injuns are after you, they're comin' in slow and easy and close, boy, or else they're ridin' past like the wind. Either way, you gotta put 'em down quick. If they're close, you lift up, shoot and drop back outta sight pronto; if they're circlin' on their devil ponies, you do the same, but you get off two shots on each. You'll soon find out they don't make easy targets just 'cause they're ridin' across your line of sight. Shoot first at the hoss, second at the man. It's important to shoot quick and sure.'

The advice had got him through the war: he had been the squad's sharpshooter, always went on ahead, picked off the sentries, then waited for the panic in the Yankee camp and dropped the soldiers as they ran about, one by one.

Now he was mighty pleased to find he hadn't lost that aptitude for accuracy and speed combined. Not having used any kind of firearm for seven years – except for on the train and at the lineshack – he had been afraid that he would not be able to get back to that old standard.

But, like riding a horse, once you've done it and felt at home in the saddle, you never forgot how.

The sixgun was different, though. He had never been one for the fast draw although he was by no means tardy when it came to sliding a Colt out of its snug leather home. And he had been a pretty good shot: maybe he mightn't hit a man exactly where he aimed, but he would hit him somewhere, and that was all that was needed most times.

Getting back the knack, though, took longer and it was well into the afternoon before he was showing any kind of satisfaction with his efforts. He not only shot at targets from stationary positions, he tried crouching – it hurt, too, *damnit!* – and running, shooting across his body, once or twice chopping at the hammer with the edge of his hand. But fanning was really only good if you were just a couple of yards from your target, though it did have an unsettling effect on any man you fired at in this manner.

He ran from rock to rock, snap-shot at his targets, mostly compressed balls of dried grass or fallen leaves now, held together with a little mud from the edge of the pool in the canyon. He wasn't hitting many dead centre but he figured if he shot within six inches of the balls, it would be a hit on a man's body. *Good enough.*

He was low on ammunition when he noticed the chill shadows filling the draw and figured it was time to quit for the day. His side was hurting and there was a little red wetness staining the bandages so he figured he had better show some good sense and go back to town.

He led the sorrel towards the steel mirror of the oval waterhole, intending to top up his saddle canteen. As he let the reins drop while he unstrapped the vessel, just before the horse lowered its muzzle into the water and disturbed the surface, Gabe saw the reflected figure up on the canyon rim.

At the same time, there was a flash of sunlight on something up there – likely field-glass lenses, he figured, pulling the protesting horse back a pace or two so he could get a better look without having to lift his face and make it obvious he had seen the watcher.

His eyebrows shot upwards and then he smiled crookedly.

The spy was moving swiftly back into the under-brush where a horse was likely waiting and he saw clearly.

Without a doubt it was Ellie Dawson.

'He's so accurate, Zac! Time after time after time! He's deadly!'

Ellie was flushed and excited, even a little shaken as she stood by the washbench beside the ZeeDee ranch house where her brother was sluicing water over his battered face and neck, careful of the bruises and cuts.

'Well, he always was a good shot,' Zac Dawson allowed, patting his sore features with a towel. 'Have to give him that.'

'But after seven years, Zac! It was frightening to watch, and *why is he doing it?* That's what scares me most!'

'Aw, take it easy, sis. You said the guns were freshly oiled when you saw 'em in the livery. My guess is he's been tunin' 'em and was takin' 'em out to sight-in.'

'And why does he need to have guns that shoot with tack-driving accuracy?' she demanded. And, giving him no chance to reply, added, 'I'll tell you why: because he's going to start killing people in this valley!'

Zac almost smiled, looking across the folds of

towel he had up near his swollen eyes. 'You still got a soft spot for him, sis?'

He thought she was going to explode, her face went so red and her bosom heaved with deep breaths, and then her eyes slitted. 'What a stupid thing to say! The man who killed our brother! Now working for another man who robbed us of our land! You want your head read, brother dear.'

Zac didn't like that and his face stiffened. But he refrained from making another comment on the subject, except to say, 'I don't think Gabe Ronan would be stupid enough to come back here and go on a killing spree.'

'Why do you say that? Everyone knows he served time that should've been shared by those hardcases he used to run with . . . Oh! I see. If anything started happening to them Gabe would be Jake Gant's first suspect.'

They moved into the house where the Indian woman cook was getting ready to serve up their supper. They went through to the parlour and sat down at the dining-table that was already set, twin candles burning as well as overhead lamps.

'But he has no love for us, either, Zac! You should've seen him! Close up, he's frightening! So hard and desperate looking! He's changed terribly.'

'A little wistful there, sis?'

She coloured and pursed her lips in that visible sign of anger he had grown to know so well over the years. 'Don't be ridiculous! Will you stop hinting at such things! He got Owen killed and he, well, he might've caused Pa to, you know.'

Zac nodded soberly. 'Yeah, Gabe's a hardcase, all right, but I guess he couldn't be anythin' else after serving that hard time in Purgatory. Milo Rafferty's leery of him. He was one of them should've done time with Gabe, I reckon. But I still don't think he's going to *start* trouble. I think he's just preparing for it if it comes his way.'

They waited while the Indian woman served the first course – some kind of beef and vegetable soup – and when she had gone, Ellie frowned and said quietly,

'You sound almost sorry for him!'

Zac smiled ruefully. 'Me? Take a good look at my face! All I'm sorry about is I didn't do as much damage to him. No, sis, I've been noticing things over the years. Johnny Keyes, for instance: he did us wrong no matter how "legal" it appears on the books. He's taking over this valley, no matter what he says different. The word is he's applied to be a Territorial Judge, and if he gets that, well, God help us all, because no one else will.'

She looked puzzled. 'I don't understand . . .'

'Keyes aims to run Paradise Valley, plain as the nose on your face, well, mine, anyway, which is a mite bigger, and kind of slanted after tanglin' with Ronan.'

'Don't joke, Zac! I – I feel scared after seeing Gabe's target practice. He was so patient, persevering. Took his time, and his tools, made fiddling adjustments, kept changing the firing mechanism or the sights until he had what he wanted. It was monotonous to watch. If you'd seen it, you'd *know* Gabe

83

Ronan has something in mind and he needs fine-shooting firearms for whatever it is.'

Her intensity got to him and he nodded soberly, reached out a hand to squeeze her forearm.

'All right, sis. Now don't worry. I'll keep a damn close eye on Ronan. And Keyes, too, I still think he's the one has Gabe worried: he can handle the others, Rafferty, the Crocketts, even Allard, the toughest of them all, but I've a hunch he figures Johnny Keyes is one big handful because he's so rich. And powerful. Money can buy a lot of things, you know.'

She nodded silently, her spoon clattering against the side of the bowl as she dipped it into the savoury-smelling soup.

At the washbench outside, just along from the dining-room window, Milo Rafferty stood with water running from his face and hands, wetting the collar of his sweaty shirt, dripping on to his boots, spotting the thick layer of dust.

He was tensed, breathing through his mouth as if afraid to make even that much noise. He had been washing up in preparation for supper – the male cook in the bunkhouse prepared the meals for the cowhands – when he had heard Ellie's intense voice in the dining-room as she told her brother about Gabe Ronan and his target practice.

By God, he thought shakily, *Gabe's gettin' ready to come after all of us, nothin' more certain!*

CHAPTER 8

GET IN FIRST!

Gabe decided to stay in town again, rather than ride across the valley to the Key spread.

Maybe it was the comfort of the bed that enticed him, or even the meals brought to the room, and the availability of a hot bath. These were luxury things he had never known a lot of during his life, but he sure could appreciate them after the spartan existence of all those years in Purgatory.

So he indulged himself in as much as he ordered a meal in his room and arranged for the big tin bath tub to be brought up in the morning when he intended to luxuriate in soap suds and hot water for an hour or so.

He had examined the wound, ignoring instructions not to undo the bandages for a couple of days. Lifting the edge of the pad carefully, he saw that one of the stitches hadn't held on the ragged edge and a little blood and clear body fluid oozed out. It was still sore but didn't look so inflamed and his flesh surrounding it felt cooler than previously.

He figured it would be all right and re-tied the covering bandages, decided to take a look around the town's night-life. Not that he had any intentions of painting the town red, but deep down one of the old urges to check out the saloons and gambling halls nudged him into curiosity. He decided not to pass up the chance although he was tired and stiff from his target pracitce.

He locked the Winchester away in a closet, buckled on the Colt and tied down the holster base, then went downstairs. Before going out the door, he stopped and checked the loads in the cylinder, thinking as he returned the Colt to leather and stepped out into the passage *Old habits die hard*.

There had been only one saloon in Providence when he had left, the Lucky Horseshoe, and with a name like that, there just had to be card tables and keno and all types of gambling. It had been a seedy place, one wall even being just a stretch of canvas on a sapling frame. But now it was painted brightly, the large horseshoe insignia on the awning over the entrance outlined with burning oil-lamps.

There was a lot of noise: tinny piano, hoarse-voiced bar gal singing some song no one was listening to, men laughing, cussing, shouting, thumping the bar for attention, 'keeps sweating and clattering trays and glasses and beer kegs. Roulette wheels clicked, dice bounced down the baize-covered tables, and players cheered or cursed, depending on how the ivory cubes settled. There were a few arguments but rugged-faced bouncers were on the alert, moved in fast and dragged troublemakers outside. Sometimes they just shoved them out into the night, other times they followed them and when they came back, the bouncers were usually sucking a split or popped knuckle or trying to dab spots of fresh blood from their shirt fronts.

It might have looked fancier and certainly was more crowded, but it seemed just as rough as the original saloon to Gabe as he made his way through the crush around the bar.

He downed a couple of iced beers – *man. they weren't just good, they were downright beautiful!* – ordered another and took the glass with him as he wandered about, watching the gamblers. He had a few bucks in his pocket left over from money given to him by Chip Allard but decided he wouldn't risk it. The games seemed OK to him but he knew the saloon would be operating at a decent profit or it wouldn't be operating at all. And how the house made a big profit was always suspect.

He jumped as someone jostled his arm and spilled some of his beer down his shirt front. Smothering a curse, he turned and the words he had been about to spit at the jostler froze on his lips.

It was big Milo Rafferty, still wearing that red bandanna instead of a hat. The Irishman grinned, showing stained, crooked teeth. His eyes were bleary and Gabe knew he had been drinking for some time.

'Did I spill your drink, boy-o?' Milo tried to execute a mock bow but there wasn't room in the crush and he earned a few curses from other drinkers. 'Well, pardon me all to hell.'

'I might just do that, Milo, this once. Buy me a fresh drink and we'll say no more about it.'

Other drinkers began to push back and make a little room around the two men, sensing possible trouble. *Free entertainment.* Milo continued to grin, swaying a little. 'Buy you another drink? Why not? We used to buy drinks for each other one time when we was friends. Long time ago.' Then the smile disappeared and the face became ugly: not that there was much handsomeness to work with in the first place. 'Nah! Changed my mind, I ain't gonna buy you nothin'!'

Rafferty leaned forward a little, thrusting his face close to Ronan's. Gabe stepped back away from the sour breath. 'OK, I'll buy. For old times' sake.'

Milo's bleary eyes slitted and he put a hand on Gabe's shoulder as the man started to push towards the bar.

'Hold up! There ain't no "old times' sake" now!'

'Well, against my better judgement, I'll still buy you a drink, Milo, what's that in your glass? Whiskey?'

Milo frowned down at the half-empty shotglass, studied it a little, then smiled crookedly. 'Yeah! Try some!'

He tossed the liquor at Ronan's face but Gabe shifted easily and it splashed on to his shoulder and the front of his shirt. Milo growled when he saw he had missed, straightened, pushing men back, lifting one tree-branch arm, fist clubbed like a hammer. 'Goddamn you, Gabe!'

Ronan tossed the remains of his beer into the

Irishman's face and drew his Colt, slammed it across the side of the man's head. Milo stood there, blinking, then grunted belatedly and sank to his knees, swaying, putting down one hand to keep from toppling.

Two bouncers came in on either side but paused warily when they saw the pistol still in Ronan's hand. 'You don't want to buy into this, fellers,' Gabe said softly, without taking his gaze from the dazed Rafferty.

'We're gonna have to if you try to use that hogleg,' one man growled, running a tongue over thick lips.

'Just give me a little room.' The gun swung casually in the direction of the bouncers and they moved back.

Ronan grabbed the red bandanna and yanked. It came away and he was shocked to see the scarred and mostly bald scalp underneath. 'Judas priest! What happened, Milo?'

Rafferty blinked up at him, but didn't speak. One of the bouncers said, 'Comanche brave caught him with his squaw, half scalped him and left him for the buzzards, but he managed to crawl back to Dawson's place and they took him in. He stayed on afterward. Had nowhere else to go.'

So that explained one thing, why Milo was riding for ZeeDee. Ronan nodded, put away the sixgun. 'Well, he always was a ladies' man. Milo, I've got no beef with you, whatever you might think. But just stay outta my way, before one of us does something he might be sorry for.'

Rafferty was regaining his senses now and staggered upright. He shook off Ronan's hand when Gabe tried to steady him, slapping it away. 'I know what you mean! You got a beef with me, all right! One from seven years ago! Like you have with the others! I know all about you practisin' with your guns out at Stillwater. You come back to get us, din' you? Well, you ain't gonna nail me! I'm tellin' you true, boy-o!'

He drove into the crowd, pushing and shoving his way towards the passage leading to the rear door. He went out, slamming it after him. The men gave Ronan plenty of room but they watched him warily as he made his way to the batwings, thinking he would have been better turning in after supper instead of coming here.

He stopped by a horsetrough, wet a kerchief and tried to wash away some of the whiskey stains, hoping the smell would go too. Then he went into a general store, bought some tobacco and papers and a couple of boxes of .44 calibre ammunition and that about exhausted his money. Carrying the parcel under his left arm, he made his way back towards the Gateway, hoping his body heat would help evaporate the smell.

He looked over the batwings of the other two saloons in town but did not enter the bar-rooms. At the second one, the Pink Lady, Milo Rafferty lurched up and roughly pushed past, holding one side of the batwing as he glared at Ronan.

'Told you to stay away from me!' Milo growled, drunker than before.

'You got it wrong, Milo, *I* told *you* to stay away from

me.' He stepped back as Milo let the door flap swing back and it slapped the parcel from his grip. 'Damn you, you butt-headed Irishman! Just leave things be, can't you?'

Rafferty snorted and lurched away into the crowded room. 'I know you're after me, you sonnabitch! You just leave me alone!'

Ronan picked up his package. Three or four cartridges had spilled and he almost had his fingers stomped on by men going in through the batwings as he picked them up. He walked to the end of the block, cut across and turned down the narrow street leading to the Gateway's side entrance stifling a yawn. His wound had caught a bony elbow in the saloon crush earlier, too, and was throbbing.

Then a gun blasted twice and bullets showered thrumming slivers from the clapboard of the building beside him. Instantly, the old instincts working, he was down on one knee, his Colt in hand and blasting at the gun-flash that came from under the stairway leading up the outside of the hotel. He heard his lead ricochet and the killer's gun triggered again.

Splinters stung his face and he crouched lower, ignoring the twinge from his wound, looked around, saw a darker patch of shadow a few yards away. But he would have to dash through a slab of light to reach it. He dropped prone, package skidding from his grip, as another shot fanned his cheek. How many shots had the killer fired? Two at first, another as he fired his own first shot, two more now – five at least. Did he only carry five loads in his gun? Or did he load every chamber?

Gabe rolled swiftly into the darker patch of shadow and had his answer – a bullet kicked gravel against the side of his neck as he scrabbled into the darkness, lurched to his knees and put three fast shots into the shadows under the stairs. The flashes from his own gun momentarily blinded him but he thought he saw another muzzle flash *from beyond the angle of the stairs. Damn! Were there two of them?*

By then running boots were pounding in the street and men were crowding into the alley, demanding to know what the hell was going on.

'It's Ronan!' someone said, recognizing Gabe as he stood up, dusting himself down, gun still cocked: he had one more cartridge left but there were men between him and the stairs now and someone called, 'Jesus wept! It's Milo Rafferty! Dead as a beef-steak!'

Just then the crowd opened out and made way for a limping Jake Gant, carrying a shotgun. His face was pain-gaunted in the sparse light but the look in his eyes as he swung the barrels of the scattergun into line with Gabe Ronan's belly was stony, penetrating.

'You just had to do it, didn't you, Gabe? You had to go after 'em!'

'What?'

'Those that left you to take the rap seven years ago, you don't aim to let 'em get away with it, huh? Milo was only the first, wasn't he?'

'Hell, I walked in here to use the side stairs and he opened up on me! I shot back in self-defence.'

'Well, you got him.'

'They tangled in the Horseshoe,' someone said. 'This Ronan kinda threatened Milo, told him to stay away or there'd be trouble.'

Others spoke up, too, and someone added, 'Milo was scared. I was in the Pink Lady and heard him say he knew Ronan was comin' after him. He was hittin' the booze.'

'Yeah, he was worried, all right,' another man said. 'Ain't much scares Milo but he was scared of this ranny.'

'Gabe, looks like you better come on down to my office. Cells ain't as comfortable as the Gateway can offer, but I reckon you'll settle in OK.' The shotgun jerked briefly. 'You want to lower that Colt hammer and leather it?'

Ronan holstered the sixgun and lifted his hands shoulder high. He was surprised to see Chip Allard pushing to the front of the crowd.

'I'll tell Johnny, Gabe. He'll get you a good lawyer if you need one.'

'He'll need one,' Gant said, sounding a little breathless. 'C'mon, move it along, Gabe. Rest of you men go about your business, but get Milo's body out of here first.'

Gant left Ronan in the cells all night and Gabe eventually went to sleep. The sheriff rattling a tin mug along the bars next morning woke him up with a start.

The sheriff opened the door, picked up a breakfast tray and handed it to Ronan as he swung his legs over the side of the bunk. It was a good meal – eggs, bacon, hot biscuits and a small pot of coffee. 'Good grub,' Gabe opined.

'Wife's a fine cook.' Gant was standing by, then squatted on the end of the bunk, crowding Gabe some. He looked tired and it was obvious his wound was hurting, the way he favoured his body movements. 'Did some askin' round last night. Seems Milo went out of his way to prod you in the Horseshoe. Old enemies, or just a guilty conscience on his part?'

'I'm not admitting anything, Jake: that's if you're trying to find out if Milo was with me on that stampede run.'

'Well, I got my own ideas about that. Thing I'm gettin' at is I heard that Milo went lookin' for you after you drifted away from the Horseshoe.'

'Could be, ran into him, literally, at the batwings of the Pink Lady, and he didn't seem friendly. He was waiting for me in the side street next to the Gateway.'

Gant sighed and nodded. 'More or less what I figured must've happened. So, we'll put it down to self-defence. But you sure made certain of him, pumpin' three bullets into him that way, one through the head.'

Gabe frowned: he was sure he hadn't hit Milo with all the shots in his last volley.

'Another thing you mightn't've thought of: rippin' that bandanna off Milo's head humiliated him in front of the crowd. The scalpin' wasn't anything he was proud of.'

Gabe nodded soberly, drinking some coffee. 'Yeah, well, no one'd told me about it. Milo always did have a hair-trigger Irish temper.'

The sheriff watched him closely. 'You got no more to say about who might've been with you when Owen

Dawson was killed?'

Gabe snapped his head up. 'No more to say. And why would you be interested? I did the time for it and it's over.'

'Well, I'd like to think so. You see, I reckon there're at least four more men in this valley who rode with you that night and let you take the rap. What I don't want is a spate of killin's in my bailiwick, with you tryin' to square things.'

'Why the hell won't anyone believe that I just came back to see the old place and to maybe settle down?'

'Likely because you were a hellion when you left and now you look like you're gonna walk right through anyone standin' in front of you if they don't get outta your way in a hurry. You got a jail look to you, Gabe, whether you like it or not. You been practisin' with your guns and a day later you kill a man in a gun duel.'

'It's just how it worked out. I didn't hunt trouble.'

Gant's eyes narrowed. 'I might halfway believe you, but I got one of the strongest hunches I can recollect that there was a damn good reason for you comin' back here. If it ain't to square with your old bunch, then it's somethin' else. Damned if I can figure what.'

Gabe stood slowly, setting the tray on the bunk. 'Don't give yourself a headache, Jake. Once I earn a little money, I'll be looking for some land. There's still prove up quarter-sections along the edge of the Hotspurs.'

'Near the Crocketts?'

Gabe smiled. 'They're too high up for my liking.

Well, can I go now?'

There was a slight hesitation before Gant nodded slowly. 'Just remember what I said: I don't want no more killin' in my town, or the valley. You savvy, Gabe?'

'I'm with you, Jake. Tell your wife that was an elegant breakfast.'

He went back to the hotel room to collect his few belongings, picked up his horse at the livery and rode out of town. An hour later, he was in the draw behind Stillwater Canyon, testing himself with the rifle.

When he was hitting the small stones and twigs he now used as targets *every* time, he set himself other challenges out to two hundred yards, with a maximum of three hundred, using the Vernier scale peep-sight to place his shots. Then he began practising with the Colt, shooting pieces of loose bark off branches: he figured if he could hit them, he would have no trouble hitting a man-size target.

He was ready for anything now, for anyone.

So let 'em come!

CHAPTER 9

LOST!

Two riders appeared around a bend in the trail that would take Ronan to the fork, one way leading to Keyes' place, the other to the Dawsons'.

Ronan hauled rein in the shadow of Knitting Needle Rock, hands resting on the saddlehorn, letting the riders approach. He knew they had seen him although the shade here was deep and black and cool.

It was Zac and Ellie Dawson and he saw the tension stiffen their shoulders when they recognized him. Zac edged a hand towards his gun-butt but Gabe kneed the sorrel into the sunlight, holding his hands out from his side.

'Relax, folks, I'm just on my way back to Key.'

'Your devil's work finished in town?' Ellie asked nastily and he smiled.

'You never used to be so bitter and childish, Ellie.'

'Shut your mouth!' snapped Zac, a mite uneasily,

still showing his bruises and cuts. 'No one talks to my sister like that!'

She quickly leaned from the saddle and placed a hand on his wrist as his hand closed about his sixgun butt. 'Zac, don't! You know you're no match for him. He, he's a cold-blooded killer!'

'Only when I have to defend myself,' Ronan said shortly. 'Guess you heard about Milo.'

'He worked for us! We're obliged to take care of his burial.'

'How come you took in a roughneck like Milo Rafferty?'

'You wouldn't understand! It's to do with decency and compassion. The man was terribly hurt. He had nowhere to go, that wound needed weeks of attention.'

'And by that time good old Milo's blarney had done its work, huh?'

She flushed but Zac said, 'He turned out to be a good cowhand, felt obliged to pay us back for helping him out.'

'Yeah, Milo was okay deep down, long as he was sober.'

'You took advantage of him, shot him while he was drunk!' Ellie snapped.

'Well, you want to believe that, OK. But Jake Gant knows different.' He nodded briefly. 'Won't keep you.'

He rode around them and Zac hipped in the saddle. 'How long you stayin'?'

Ronan didn't slow down or look around. 'Till I'm ready to leave.'

They watched him ride to the bend and pass out of sight.

'He's frightening,' Ellie opined and her brother looked at her sharply.

'Ye-ah, he's tough all right. But, I dunno, there's somethin' about him I can't figure. He knows he's not wanted here but he stays on. *Somethin's* keeping him here and I'd sure like to know what.'

The girl's lips compressed. 'Milo was only the first! You'll see: Gabe Ronan is, is vindictive and bitter and he's here to make trouble for people! *That's* what's keeping him here: the chance to make more trouble!'

'Well, while he was a hellion before, there never was a lot of real harm in him; no one really got hurt. Till Owen, of course.'

'You're a fool Zac Dawson, if you believe Gabe Ronan is here for anything else but cold-blooded murder!'

She lashed at her mount with her quirt and spurred away, bringing the horse to a gallop swiftly and racing it towards town.

Frowning slightly, Zac Dawson followed at a more sedate pace. He knew his sister pretty well and he could have sworn there were tears welling in her eyes when she rode away.

Johnny Keyes was giving instructions for the next day's work to his wrangler and a couple of cowhands when Ronan rode back into the ranch yard. Keyes looked up and watched closely as Gabe slowed his mount by the corrals, dismounted a little stiffly and started to loosen the cinch-strap. Chip Allard came hurrying up from the blacksmith's forge, still carrying fire-blackened tongs.

'You need a hand?'

Ronan shook his head at the ramrod, glanced at Johnny Keyes who was still holding a workbook, the three ranch hands waiting patiently.

'All right if I still use that room, Johnny?'

Keyes smiled. 'Hell, it's yours, told you that. Long as you like. When you feel ready to work, let me know. There's a job for you here, like I said. Oh, Bill Renny's made some new grass lassos. Chip'll get one for you.'

Ronan thanked him and off-saddled, taking his rifle scabbard with him as he started for the house. Chip fell in beside him, tossing the fire-tongs into the barn doorway.

'Told Johnny you might be in trouble but he said to wait and see what happened this mornin'.' He grinned and punched Ronan lightly on the shoulder. 'Still fast-talkin' I guess if you got past Jake Gant.'

'Nothing to hold me for,' Gabe said, sitting on the porch steps. Chip sat beside him and offered him the makings and both men built cigarettes. They were smoking when Keyes dismissed the wrangler and his pards and came up. He sat on the step below the others, took out a cheroot and lit up.

'Chip tell you why I didn't send you in a lawyer last night?'

Gabe nodded. 'That's OK. I knew I was in the right.'

Keyes smiled. 'Don't always count, but guess it did this time.' He gestured to the rifle. 'See you've oiled it again. Been practisin'?'

'Fine-tuning my shooting, working up a little speed.'

A frown fleetingly creased Keyes' forehead and Chip Allard looked quickly at his boss. 'Thinking of hunting or something?' Keyes asked casually.

Gabe shrugged. 'Seven years is a long time not handling firearms, and I'm back where a man needs to know such things now by the looks of things.'

'So it's just a precaution?' Johnny asked.

'That, or something I *want* to do. I always liked guns as you recollect.'

'Sure, our sharpshooter and pathfinder, you must've killed more Yankees than the rest of the troop put together, Gabe.' This was Chip speaking and he grinned, sounded like the memories were to his liking: his specialty had been strangling sentries.

Gabe's face gave nothing away. 'Guess it's an inbred thing. I'd had an itching all those years in Purgatory to start carrying my own firearms again.'

Johnny Keyes gestured to the rifle and the sixgun. 'Well, you've got 'em and I guess Milo was just plumb loco to try you out.'

'Aw, maybe I pushed him a little. Didn't mean to: when I whipped that bandanna off his head, didn't know about the scalping. I guess that and the booze put him on the prod.'

Keyes pursed his lips as he blew out a plume of smoke. 'Maybe he figured *your* prodding was deliberate. That you *wanted* him to call you out so you'd have an excuse to shoot him.'

Ronan's eyes were steady, cool, as he crushed out

his cigarette and stood up. 'Guess I'll go wash up for supper.'

'Sure, it won't be long,' Keyes said.

They watched him go into the house and Chip asked soberly, 'What d'you think? Reckon he deliberately went after Milo?'

'You asked around, didn't you?'

Allard nodded. 'Couldn't get anythin' clear. They tangled, but I'd say, if anything, Milo pushed it.'

Keyes pursed his lips thoughtfully, didn't answer.

'I mean, if he *is* gonna come after us one by one, Johnny, where do you and me fit on the list? We were always closest to him.'

'You were, anyway, but I been thinkin' about that.' He paused for a few moments then said thoughtfully, 'Take him with you tomorrow with some of the boys, go look for mustangs and any mavericks you can catch. Take Gabe deep into that back country above Deacon Plains and lose him.'

Chip blinked. '*Lose* him?'

Keyes nodded slowly. 'Yeah. If he is gonna be a pain in the ass and come after us, I want to get his measure. He was a damn good scout once. Let's see how good he is now after hard-time in jail, when he's put in a situation where he has to rely on just himself. This'll be a kinda trial.'

'Hell, Gabe could find his way out of a graveyard from six feet under; he won't stay lost for long!'

Keyes smiled thinly. 'Maybe just long enough . . .'

'And what's that mean?'

But the rancher didn't answer, flicked away the butt of his cheroot, stood up and went into his office through the narrow door just along the porch.

Chip Allard smoked his cigarette all the way down till it burned his fingers. He flung it from him with an oath before starting for the wash-bench, puzzled.

The hell did Johnny Keyes have in mind?

Gabe Ronan didn't really feel like riding the range on a round-up chore, but Chip jollied him along and made a few remarks about 'fellers who had just finished a seven-year holiday were takin' a slew of settlin' down: must've had it too soft for too long.'

Gabe shook his head slowly, smiling. 'You damn shyster! Always did have a slick tongue and knew just how to prod a man.'

'That what I was doin'?' Chip seemed genuinely surprised. 'Hell, I was just talkin', but if it kinda gets to you, makes you want to join us workers . . . Welcome!'

'OK! Damn you!' Ronan scowled but he sounded amiable enough as he reached for his clothes, and his gun rig. 'Hell, it's not even proper daylight!'

'Will be about the time we finish breakfast. C'mon, Gabe, you used to like startin' early.'

'That was before they woke me every morning at 4.30 and shoved a fourteen-pound sledge in my hand. Most days there was no breakfast at all. Early grows old after that.'

Chip sobered as Ronan finished dressing and buckled on his sixgun. 'Yeah, well, maybe I was bein' a bit too much smart-ass. Musta been hell in there.'

'Good introduction to the real place, I reckon. C'mon, I'm hungry now.'

But he wasn't really. Fact was he felt kind of fever-

ish and when he went to the privy after eating breakfast with the other Key cowhands in the dogrun
between the kitchen and bunkhouse, he eased the
bandages covering his wound gently aside. He tightened his lips, swore under his breath.

The edge where the stitch had pulled through
looked inflamed and swollen. He thought there might
even be a little pus there – all of which meant infection.

That was likely why he felt feverish: his face was hot
but dry to the touch, a sure sign of incipient fever.
Well, a few hours working in the outdoors might help
sweat it out of his system, he decided, but not really
believing it.

He joined a bunch of ten other cowhands and
Chip Allard gathering at the corrals and, soon after,
Chip led them out of the yard, riding towards the
Hotspurs.

Johnny Keyes watched from his bedroom, where
he was standing by the window in a silk robe, a
cheroot in one hand, the other holding a cup of
coffee. He watched with narrowed eyes as, when the
riders reached the creek, Chip broke them up into
three groups. Two lots set off west and south, Chip,
with Gabe and Bill Renny, rode into the hills where
the timber grew thickly.

Keyes smiled slowly: Chip was going to dump Gabe
in the wildest part of the Hotspurs. Over the years,
three men and a woman had disappeared in that country. There was such a tangle of vegetation that it closed
right over and virtually blotted out the sky so a man
couldn't rightfully get a good sight of the sun or stars
at night. A horse wasn't much good in there because

there was little room for such a big animal to manoeu-vre. But there were wolves in the general area, even the odd black bear, a small variety but a savage one, not to mention snakes in the thickets that were at every turn.

Water, of course, was scarce, virtually non-existent, food more so unless you were an Indian and knew for certain sure which berries and wild fruits were safe to eat and which were deadly poisonous.

Johnny Keyes grinned as he drained his coffee.

Good old Chip knew the best – or worst – spots to abandon Gabe Ronan. It would be interesting to see if Gabe could make it out fast by himself. To be on the safe side, he would have a couple of men standing by to go search for him if it seemed that Ronan was not going to make it. That would cover him with Jake Gant who, more often than not, was just as big a pain in the butt as Ronan was proving to be. If only he could believe Gabe wasn't here to collect scalps. He sobered, thinking it might have been better if they had hanged Gabe Ronan seven years ago or given him a life stretch and he wouldn't be giving anyone goosebumps and ulcers by turning up where he wasn't wanted.

It was mighty hard work chasing mavericks in that thick timber. Most times they didn't even see the wild animals, just found sign by way of hoof marks, dung, tufts of hair or a strip of hide caught on broken twigs, or scratchings in tree bark from the long horns.

Chip or Renny would get all excited, yelling, 'This way!' or 'There goes the son of a bitch! After him, Gabe!'

Gabe was slow, much slower than he used to be, of

course, but felt uneasy and out of synch somehow in this close-fitting, semi-dark timber. The brush was thick and the sorrel protested as it tore at its chest and forelegs, scraped its rump and ripped Gabe's trousers, too. He should have asked for a pair of leather chaps but figured the round up would be in a more accessible place than this. He tried to talk to Chip about it but Allard was intent now on running down the mavericks and didn't pause to listen, merely pointed left, shouting, 'Jesus, Gabe! Open your eyes, man! You're lettin' one get past you!'

He was dizzy from wheeling this way and that. The sorrel was breathing hard, scratched and battered, just as its rider was. By noon they had choused out only seven mavericks, two of which were heifers. The rest were snorting, brush-wild beasts who wanted nothing more than to run their horns through horse or rider when they came within reach. They used ropes between two horsemen to drag the bellowing, bucking beasts to the holding pens that had been prepared. Privately, Gabe reckoned the poles weren't going to hold under the ramming, kicking shennanigans of the penned cattle.

'We'll skip lunch,' Chip said, spitting dried leaves and twigs and dust after a fall from his mount. 'Press on and get as many as we can penned up before sundown, camp here overnight, maybe collect a few more mavericks before we haze 'em back to the ranch.' He frowned. 'You feelin' all right, Gabe? You look kinda flushed, slow to react.'

'Hadn't noticed,' Gabe said quietly. But he didn't feel in the least hungry: his body was overheated and he had a raging thirst, his canteen almost empty. There were no easily accessible streams or waterholes in here according to Chip. 'Could have a touch of fever,' he admitted finally. 'Got a helluva headache. Not thinking too clearly, either.'

'Well, hell that ain't too good. You get any worse let me know.'

Gabe didn't want to appear weak. 'I'll be OK. Some cool water'd help.' All canteens were nearly empty.

Once Renny rode up alongside, sweaty, sober-look-ing. 'I usually get paid for makin' them lariats.' He nodded to the new rope in Gabe's hands. 'I'm kinda short right now.'

'Have to owe you, Bill. I'm not short, I'm broke.'

Renny scowled, muttered something and rode back to work. Gabe frowned: the cowboy looked mighty riled.

Chip and Renny yelled at him several times when he found himself in thick, clawing brush and they needed him to head off a running maverick in a hurry. The sorrel was in a mess, torn up, sweating. Finally, Chip told him to head on down to a patch of brush and into a thicket where there might be an old waterhole – not sweet water, mostly full of dead leaves and insects. If he could find it, it might help.

'Dunk your head, wake yourself up.'

'You saying I'm not pulling my weight?' Gabe felt irritable, short-tempered, knew the fever was working on him.

'See if you can find that waterhole and come on back, Gabe. We better just make a couple more runs, lock down the pens, and head back to Key after all, I reckon. You don't look too dusty. Need a hand, old pard?'

Chip knew damn well that would get a snappy reply and he wasn't disappointed. Still muttering, Gabe forced the weary, scratched-up sorrel through the brush, fighting thorny vines that tore his clothes and flesh. Chip wanted his head read sending him into a place like this and maybe *he* needed his head read for complying.

But it was too late to turn around and the thought of water, slushy or not, was beginning to take over his thinking. He pushed on, trying to turn his thoughts from water and fever. Then the press of brush and trees demanded his concentration for which he was grateful. But, with a lurch in his belly, he suddenly realized that he had lost direction. His teeth were chattering and he was both hot and cold at the same time. The trees were crowding him, making the exhausted sorrel nervous. It was probably picking up some of his own anxious vibrations. Finally, he faced the truth:

He didn't know where the hell he was; he couldn't hear Chip or Renny, or even the damn mavericks! The trees were so thick overhead he couldn't see more than small ragged patches of sky.

For the first time since he was ten years old, Gabe Ronan realized he was lost.

He felt so bad that he didn't even recognize that wild, tearing feeling inside him as rising panic.

CHAPTER 10

HANGMAN'S KNOT

Shep had always been the Crockett who couldn't sleep well. Which probably accounted for his perpetual sour mood and quick temper.

He figured it was well after midnight when he got out of his smelly bunk, not bothering to be quiet about rummaging for his boots and pulling them on with heavy sighs, stomping his feet in firmly.

'Goddamn you, Shep!' growled Ringo sleepily. 'If I could reach the skillet I'd bend it over your goddamn head!'

'Ah, go back to sleep you lucky bastard!'

Shep groped for his pipe and shag tobacco and stomped to the door, using a boot to kick it open. As usual, it screeched across the uneven flagstones on the porch. He almost smiled as he heard his brother mutter another curse.

Shep sat on the stoop and filled his pipe, got it going, and only then looked at the night. A half-moon was heeled over in the east, still rising. But it didn't dim the sky full of stars, brilliant, twinkling, a thin blade of fire trailing from an earth-bound meteor. Supposed to be lucky, seeing a falling star, too bad one hadn't hit him on the head long ago and then he might be leading an entirely different life from this one.

Not that it was so bad. Bit lonely way up here on the high slopes, with only ugly old Ringo, an occasional whore and a couple of dogs to look at, but they lived well enough, guiding a few rustlers and their herds or the odd man on the dodge, up to and through the high pass.

Of course they didn't do it for nothing and had soon learned that if a man was running from a killing he would pay five or even ten times as much as some feller just trying to get away from a vengeful wife or some gal he had done wrong.

Gant knew what they were up to but they were too smart for him to catch them redhanded. Still one day it could happen and . . .

Suddenly he sat up straight, pipe poised just short of his open mouth.

'By God! That's cows I hear!' he said aloud, jumping to his feet. He listened again, head on one side, and when he knew he wasn't mistaken he stormed back into the hut, yelling at Ringo.

His brother came fully awake, heart hammering, blinking. 'What in tarnation are you. . . ?'

'Damn you, Ringo! Why din' you tell me someone was bringin' through a herd tonight?'

There was a silence, broken only by Shep's angry breathing, then Ringo said, 'Ain't no one due, damnit, Shep, use your eyes! It's half-moon tonight!

110

I ain't loco enough to let anyone drive through here at half-moon!'

It stopped Shep. Ringo was right: it was only on moonless nights that they guided stolen herds to and through the high pass.

'Then who the hell? Judas, Ringo! There's cows comin'! I ain't been asleep so I ain't dreamin' You come listen.'

Reluctantly and muttering, Ringo limped to the open door and he had only taken one step out on to the stone-flagged porch, jumping a little at the coldness against his bare feet, when he heard the muted bawling of cattle down the slope.

'Christ! Who the hell is it?'

Both Crocketts hurried back inside, pulled on trousers over their long johns, their boots and hats and grabbed their guns. By the time they got back outside, they could see the shadowy movement of cattle across the slopes.

And the cows were strung out, some starting to browse on the lush high-country clover patches, others just flopping down. They weren't being driven; they were *wandering*. Which made it even more of a puzzle.

The brothers looked at each other. Shep said slowly, 'Looks like there ain't anyone hazin' 'em along! They musta just drifted up here.'

'This high up the mountain? Like hell they did! C'mon, let's git on down there and see what's happenin'!'

Their guns were cocked as they stumbled down the dim slopes. The cows were obviously used to

111

humans for they didn't bellow or run away as they approached. Then Ringo leaned over one that was sitting down, chewing its cud, and strained to see the brand in the strengthening half-moon light.

'Judas priest!' he said, rearing back, jaw hanging. 'These are *Key* steers!'

'Jesus! We're dead men if Johnny finds 'em on our land!'

'Damn right! But I reckon we better prepare for some visitors, Johnny Keyes or not. This has a damn bad smell about it, brother-mine, *damn* bad!'

The Crocketts waited, battened-down inside their cabin. It had an outward appearance of a slapped-together shack, but inside was lined with narrow logs, the doors sheathed with sheet-iron.

They knew that, in their business, sooner or later they would be besieged here and had prepared for it. Now both men's mouths were dry. It was Ringo who broke out the jug of syrupy corn liquor they had taken in payment for guiding a desperate fugitive through the pass a couple of weeks ago. It was special stuff, stolen from the cellars of none other than the Gateway Hotel in Providence.

'Might's well limber up on somethin' that's gonna stick to our innards,' Ringo said, taking the first long draught. 'Someone's bound to come after them cows and . . .'

'Ease up, damnit!' snapped Shep, nerves on edge. 'My ticker's bouncin' around like a ten-dollar whore! Gimme the jug!'

They had each taken three hefty swigs before, a

trifle blearily, Shep looked out the front shutter and hissed in a shaky voice, 'Someone's comin'!'

'Bet it ain't Santy Claus!' slurred Ringo, giggling mildly.

'You lay off that stuff or you won't be able to hit the side of a barn with a shotgun!'

'That so?' Ringo asked, settling at his window and sighting down his rifle barrel. A shadow moved at the edge of the timber and he fired. The noise slammed at their ears in the closed-down cabin.

Shep, looking out, saw a man and horse floundering on the slope, the rider heaving to his feet and hugging one side as he ran for the deeper shadow of the trees. Shep didn't see anyone else so took a shot at the stumbling man to hurry him along. 'You only got his hoss, and that was just a winger!'

The horse whinnied, heaved awkwardly to its feet and ran after its rider. 'Who is he?' asked Ringo, reaching for the jug again.

Shep intercepted him. 'Leave it be, Ringo! We dunno who's out there or how many! We could be in real trouble!'

Ringo Crockett blinked. 'Hell, whoever's out there is the ones in trouble! We'll shoot 'em right outta their britches. Gimme that!' He wrested the jug free from Shep and tilted it, spilling some down his chin.

Shep figured he might miss out altogether if he didn't get his share now and a grunting, cursing tug-of-war started just as gunfire crashed outside and bullets thudded into the walls, a couple *clunking* as they struck the sheet-iron lining on the door.

'Might be more'n one by the sounds of that!'

exclaimed Shep, hugging the floor now.

'I'll teach the sonuver a lesson!' Ringo threw up his shutter recklessly and raked the timber with four fast shots. Shep added three more and then both grabbed for the jug, which was a lot lighter than previously.

'Go on home, whoever you are!' roared Ringo. 'We is all snugged-up in here. We'll wear you down by sun-up! *Git!*'

There was silence outside and the brothers slumped against the wall, chuckling stupidly as they passed the jug back and forth until it was empty. Their heads were really spinning by this time and Shep suddenly frowned.

'Long time since – we – heard from – them bastards outside – pard . . . Loooooong time!'

He struggled up and lifted his shutter slightly just as he smelled smoke and the first blazing shingle tumbled down from the roof, missing him by a foot, spattering sparks.

'Aw, hell!' Ringo growled. 'We beefed-up the walls but forgot about the goddamn roof!'

They had indeed forgotten and in only a few minutes most of the roof and its supports were ablaze, starting to cave in, large pieces crashing into the fortified room. Staggering, choking in the smoke, eyes watering, they fumbled at the door's bar, flung it open. The rush of fresh air sent flaming shingles flying about like giant fireflies and the drunken Crocketts staggered out into the night. They tried to spread out but both turned towards each other and tangled. They shoved and pushed and swore, trying to unlimber their rifles.

Then flame stabbed under the trees, again and again, and Shep and Ringo fell awkwardly, clothes bullet-torn and bloody.

The echoes of the gunfire died away across the slopes. Some of the cattle were up and running, bawling, putting distance between themselves and the cabin that was burning and roaring like a Roman candle.

Some blazing shingles and twigs fell across the bodies, scorching the clothing. Ringo was past caring and didn't stir, blood trickling from his mouth. But Shep, coughing and wheezing, tried to grab his gun.

A scuffed riding boot pinned his hand to the ground and a rifle barrel with a curl of smoke at the muzzle rapped him lightly across the head.

'Leave it. I got me a good rope here I been wantin' to try out, Shep. You just been elected.'

Shep had enough life left in him to feel the gritty noose settle over his head and draw in tight against his sweaty throat. And when the hangman's knot dug in under his left ear, he knew it was way too late even to cry out.

Ronan had no idea where he was or what had happened to him. He tried hard to concentrate but other thoughts insisted on intruding. Thoughts that took him back seven years to that one night he could never forget.

His brain felt like scrambled eggs, full of overlapping memories, murmurings and distant shouts. A chill shook him even as sweat drenched his aching body. Then the pulsating redness behind his eyes settled into a pale grey and images began to form.

It had started out to be a night of fun, but somewhere a cog slipped and all hell broke loose.

They had taken on a load of booze in the railroad survey camp on the far side of the Hotspurs and it was pure, aged-for-a-day rotgut. Chip Allard was sick twice on the ride home and Milo let himself fall into Gabriel Creek, floundering in the water in an effort to sober up. No success.

The Crocketts didn't seem so affected as the rest, but they were from Kentucky, had grown up on moonshine and sourmash. Johnny Keyes was almost sober: as usual, he hadn't put away much of the liquor. Gabe Ronan was happy: he knew he was drunk but he felt basically OK. No upset guts, although his head was buzzing, but he felt more like singing than throwing up.

He cleared his throat and started on the trail driver's version of 'Buffalo Gals' but the others shouted at him to *shut up*! They had already heard fifty-one verses and that was *enough*!

But Gabe was in too good a mood to be put off. 'Well, come on, you sorry bunch of knotheads! I thought we were out for *fun*! You look like you're going to a funeral!'

'I'll git a funeral goin' right soon you don't quit that shoutin'!' growled Milo holding his head. 'Where are we? Back in the valley yet?'

'Just about,' Johnny Keyes said, the only one with his wits about him. 'Go through that cutting, we'll get there.'

'Whoa! That's crossin' Dawson land!' slurred Chip Allard, gargling with creek water.

'So? It'll save us miles. Anyway, to hell with Zachary Dawson. Too goddamn big for his boots. 'Then Keyes' voice took on a note of cunning. 'But not for much longer! I got his measure! I can get me a look at the land register now and I know how to cut Mr Bigshot Dawson down to size.'

'Not interested,' cut in Gabe. 'Let's cut across ZeeDee land. Hey! How's about we roust 'em a little? Make 'em think Injuns are hitting their herds! Scare the pants off 'em! eh?'

'Wouldn' mind scarin' the pants off that Ellie!' opined Ringo Crockett and reeled back as Ronan rammed his horse into him, knocking him into the creek.

'You watch your mouth, Ringo!'

Gabe fought his horse to a standstill, aware that they were all staring at him now.

'Uh-*huh*!' said Keyes smiling crookedly. 'So it *was* you I saw riding along the river with her the other afternoon?'

Ronan wheeled his mount, spurring away, yelling, 'C'mon, you bunch of old grannies! Let's liven up the old ZeeDee!'

They were drunk enough and reckless enough to follow and when they came upon a Dawson herd penned in a fattening-up pasture, they readily went along with Gabe's mischief when he said, 'Now a few wild Injun yells and a leetle gunfire oughta tumble them uppitty Dawsons outta their beds and spoil their sleep!'

'Count me in!' Milo Rafferty bawled, fumbling for his sixgun.

'You'll give old Zachary a heart attack!' warned Chip Allard.

'That's good enough reason for me!' Johnny Keyes allowed and groped for his own Colt.

Then they froze as a rider came out of the night, closing with them. As soon as he spoke, they all recognized the voice of Owen, the youngest Dawson, the spoilt brat of the family.

'Sounds like you're out for some hellraisin', gents,' said Owen a trifle nervously. He was just out of his teens, a pouting youth, used to having his own way simply by demanding or throwing a tantrum until his wishes were granted just to placate him. He could be damn bossy, too.

'Aw, hell!' allowed Shep Crockett who had no love for any of the Dawsons. 'Now the spoil-sport has to turn up, like a bad smell at the supper table!'

There were growls from the others, and they were all surprised when Owen kneed his mount closer.

'I ain't tryin' to spoil things for you boys, 'fact, I'll help you do whatever you were plannin'.'

The group studied him in silence, their scepticism obvious as Johnny Keyes said, mockingly, 'What's happened, kid? Had another spat with the Old Man? He won't give you something you want?' Owen pouted now, his horse restless. 'Go throw your tantrum somewhere else, kid, we don't want you.'

'But maybe you *need*, me!' Owen said with a petulant snarl.' I *could* raise the alarm. Hey, wait up! Only kiddin'! Yeah, Pa an' me've had a fallin' out. He *made* me come ride nighthawk on this here herd! I wanted to go to the dance in Tolliver! Had me a little

Mormon immigrant gal lined up. Zac don't have to do half the goddamn chores I have to! The Old Man makes me work harder than the damn ranch hands and I've had a bellyful. You wanna play Injuns? Scatter the herd? Well, let's do it!'

They knew that if Owen did raise the alarm, Zachary would throw the entire ZeeDee crew against them and they were in no shape for anything like that. But none of them had a chance to think beyond that point, for Owen, when he finished speaking, wheeled away, raking his mount with his spurs, yelling like a Comanche with the bellyache, firing his sixgun into the air.

In seconds, all hell broke loose and the wild bunch were only too willing to join in and add their contribution to the chaos. The startled herd lurched to its feet, bawling, snorting, rudely awakened by the yelling men and hammering gunfire. Rafferty's big horse reared up in fright, came down with raking forefeet. It ripped into the head of a steer, taking out one eye. The animal went loco, slashing with its horns at everything within reach, snorting and bellowing in pain as it plunged through the milling cattle, gouging, slobbering steam and silver threads of saliva, trying to climb over the backs of the others.

Gabe yelled himself hoarse, had a sudden urge to empty his bladder, but forced himself to ignore it. He was caught up in the rush of excitement and violence now as the herd's thunder shook the very earth beneath his mount. Lights were appearing in the distant ranch house and bunkhouse and he thought he could hear vague shouting. His gun was hot and empty. Somehow he fumbled in fresh loads, riders, screaming drunkenly, flashing past on one side, the terrorized cattle on the other. The din was terrible but it seemed worthwhile to him at that moment as he wheeled, spurred his mount alongside mad-eyed steers, shooting and yelling.

Young Owen was riding recklessly, face lit up with excitement and the knowledge he was showing Zachary Dawson he wouldn't be pushed around by him or anyone else. Then his horse snorted and tried to rear in pain, blood gushing from a great slash across its neck and chest. The crazy steer's horn ripped into Owen's leg and then both man and animal went down under the mashing, blurred, pounding hoofs of the stampeding cattle.

Instinctively, Gabe tried to haul rein, wrenching his horse's head aside, shouting Owen's name. But his horse's left forefoot broke through the earth into a gopher hole and the snapping bone sounded like a pistol shot even above the din and thunder.

Then he found himself twisting, losing his sixgun, the sea of white-eyed slavering heads and heaving backs and tossing horns rushing to meet him. There was a bright explosion and a jar that felt as if his spine had been torn from his body.

Then nothing, black, spinning *nothing*.

He didn't even hear someone yell: 'Here come the Dawsons! Let's get the hell outta here!'

CHAPTER 11

GABE'S REASON

The sounds of the stampede had faded from Gabe Ronan's fever-tortured brain when he felt ready to open his eyes. He didn't know how long it had been since he had relived that hellish night in his fevered mind.

There was this strange feeling that he had been somewhere, locked away, or, leastways, deprived of all voluntary movement. And there was weakness, yet also a feeling of returning strength, in his drained body.

But he did feel *better* though, better from what? An illness? Could be . . . He opened his eyes.

His hands clawed into fabric as he stared up at a pinewood ceiling from which twin oil lamps swung, burning now but turned very low. His throat was dry and his tongue felt as if it was stuck to the roof of his mouth. He made a gurgling noise and lowered his eyes at a sound coming from somewhere beneath the level of his gaze.

Someone came around the bed in which he was lying, dimly seen in the deep orange glow of the lamps. Blinds were drawn over the windows. He blinked, shaking his head once as he tried to clear his vision.

'Decided to join us again?'

He felt his brow furrow deeply as he squinted and stared at Ellie Dawson. *She was smiling!* A small, cool hand pressed gently against his clammy forehead and held him against the pillow without effort. She looked deep into his eyes and then he felt her hand moving beneath the sheets, feeling for his heartbeat. The smile, which had faded a little, returned. 'You're much better, Gabe, the fever has broken.'

He tried to move and grimaced, reaching weakly across to his bandaged side.

'Your wound was infected, irritated by dirt and twigs, even some kind of dead insect. Lord knows what you've been doing. But I've bathed it well with hot water and Eusol, set a piece of yarn I boiled up first in the wound itself to drain it. You'll be on your feet in no time, I imagine.'

He stared at her, frowning, and she suddenly sat on the edge of the bed, took his hand between hers and stroked it as she spoke softly, eyes glistening. 'Oh, Gabe! What have they done to you? All those dreadful scars on your back! Others on your shoulders and neck, the backs of your legs! You must've been beaten within an inch of your life.'

'Several times,' he croaked. She got him a drink, turned out the lamps, and raised the blinds part-way, letting in bright daylight that had an afternoon look to it.

'Oh, my God! And we – *I*—' Her hand went up and pushed her hair off her face and he saw twin trickles of tears coursing down her face. She paused. 'You – you talked and shouted a lot in your fever, almost all about that night seven years ago when Owen was killed.'

'It's been on my mind a long time. I wanted to explain to you.'

She took his hand again, clasping it, lifting the back against her damp cheek. 'Gabe, I was awful to you the other day! I-I'm sorry. I-I've hated you, you know.'

He smiled. 'Kinda got that impression.'

'Yes, well, you took the blame for everything and that included Owen's death, but after what you said in your fever.' She heaved a deep breath. 'It seems Owen was to blame for his own death! He was just acting his normal, spoilt, spiteful self!' The dark hair fell across her face again as she shook her head jerkily. 'But what I don't understand is *why* you took all the blame! Went to jail and let the others stay free.'

'Complicated. Folk already suspected, of course. I just didn't confirm it.'

'Knowing you that's not surprising,but, please tell me why, Gabe?'

'Johnny Keyes saved my life.'

'You mean, during the war he—?'

He nodded. 'If I'd named just one of the others, it would've been the same as naming them all, because we were a group, including Johnny. He carried me over his shoulders for twenty miles through Yankee-held country and got me back to our lines, nursed me all the way. I'd've died without his help.'

She took a little time to digest it, nodded slowly. 'Yes, you are the kind of man who would remember such a thing and I admire you for it. But the others? None of them is much good, Gabe! I know we felt sorry for Milo and I have to admit he didn't seem all that bad at times but he was, essentially, still a hard-case. Like the rest.'

'Milo, the Crocketts, Chip Allard, Johnny – we were all in the same troop. An advance squad clearing the way for the main company. We lived in each other's pockets, on patrol, in wilderness camps, under fire and when we were on leave or found time to whoop-it-up, together. We knew *everything* about each other.'

'Camaraderie!'

'Guess that's the name for it. One time, someone suggested we take an oath, to be loyal to each other forever, no matter what, to be man enough to stand alone in any trouble we brought on ourselves and keep the others out of it. You know the kind of fool-ish things grown men do at times, specially after a few drinks, though we were only half grown, I guess. But I took that oath seriously, Ellie. I tried to explain it to you once, up at Stillwater Canyon.'

She nodded soberly. 'I remember – I remember almost every word you've ever spoken to me, Gabe.' He didn't look away and her teeth tugged at her bottom lip. 'Oh, I've been such a fool! And you came back to me, didn't you? That's the real reason you returned to the valley, isn't it? For *me*!' He was silent for so long that she flushed and said, haltingly, 'I-I guess that sounds full of ego, but that's why you're here isn't it? And I don't deserve your consideration!'

'Yeah, I came back to see you, Ellie, maybe with some notion of settling down here. Preferably with you, but just to live in the valley and know you were nearby, to see you occasionally, would've been enough.'

She made no attempt to restrain the tears now and, sobbing, threw her arms about his neck, pressing herself against his chest. After a little while he slipped one arm about her shoulders and she seemed to settle in against him like she was a part of him, where she belonged.

It seemed a long time later, the room filling with sunlight now, that he asked quietly, voice still a little hoarse, 'How did I get here? I guess "here" *is* ZeeDee?'

She nodded, pushed back from him, took out a delicate-looking scented kerchief and mopped at her face, blew her nose genteely.

'One of our men found you, Chuck Ariel, not sure if you know him. Your poor horse came out of some scrub with you reeling in the saddle, the reins looped about your wrists to keep you from falling, clothes in shreds. The sorrel was dreadfully cut up and had three-inch thorns sticking out of it. One eye was badly damaged; it must've just ploughed straight through all those thickets.'

Gabe tried to take it in, frowning. 'Where was this?'

'Halfway down the slope, far to the north of the last bend of Gabriel Creek, wild country, backing up from our pastures.' A little bitterly, she added, 'Land Johnny Keyes obviously didn't want when he stole Deacon Plains from us! Chuck had heard shooting way up the slope. He didn't know if you'd been involved, but you were in such a state, that he brought you straight here.'

Gabe's lips twitched. 'Bet Zac was happy about that!'

'Well, maybe not *too* happy. But when I worked on you and saw those awful prison scars, I began to realize just what a terrible time you'd been through.' She paused, taking a deep breath in an effort to control a rising sob. He spoke so as to take her mind off it.

'I got lost up in the Hotspurs, working mavericks with Chip and a cowpoke named Renny. When they saw I was running a fever, Chip sent me to look for water but I got lost. Can't recall much: felt real bad, wrapped the reins round my wrists, think I might've fired off my guns to get Chip's and Renny's notice – not sure – next thing, I woke up here.'

'That sorrel was one Johnny Keyes bought off us one time. Zac sold him several mounts. Most animals when they're hurt make for somewhere they know is safe; I guess your sorrel just ploughed on through that scrub regardless, instinct telling him it would eventually lead to ZeeDee, where he had been treated well.'

'Or maybe he was making for Johnny Keyes' place?

The horse has been there for a spell from what I gather.'

'Perhaps it was treated better here. Chip Allard's not noted for his kindness to horses.'

That was true: many times Gabe had butted heads with Chip over the years about the way he treated his mounts. Chip didn't like it but passed it off well enough. 'Anyway, seems I've got the sorrel to thank, as well as you, Chuck and Zac.'

She smiled faintly. 'I don't think I'd worry too much about thanking Zac: he doesn't want you here at all.'

Gabe nodded, weary now. He noticed a strange look on Ellie's face. There was a hint of worry mixed with puzzlement there. He asked what was on her mind.

'Chip Allard should've known there was no chance of finding water in those thickets, Gabe.'

His eyes narrowed a little. 'He said I *might* find water but it'd be full of insects and leaves, more like slush, I guess. But I was burning up so much I didn't care if it was just plain mud, long as it was cool.'

She shifted uncomfortably. 'I know those thickets quite well, Gabe. Pa used to get a lot of maverick heifers out of them years ago, soon after the breeding season. It was a fine place for the cows to hide their calves from the wolves. *Because there's no water there to bring the wolves in!* They're all round the edges, but not in the thicket itself.'

Ronan shook his head slowly. 'All I know is what Chip said. He'd have no reason for sending me in there just to get lost.'

127

She frowned. 'No,I suppose not, but it is strange.' Then she smiled again. 'But you're safe and on the road to recovery now, so that's all that matters.'

They both tensed and Ellie stood quickly as they heard the front door open and footsteps coming down the hall. Zac Dawson came in swiftly, looking straight at Gabe.

He grunted. 'Still here, eh? Hope you're feelin' better, because sooner you're outta here, the happier I'll be.'

'Zac!' Ellie said sharply. 'For heaven's sake! His fever only broke a couple of hours ago!'

Zac was still looking hard at Gabe. 'You have any kinda beef with the Crocketts?'

Gabe frowned. 'Well, they weren't pleased to see me, like just about everyone else in the valley. I think Shep and Ringo have a guilty conscience because they let me take the rap for them and the others, afraid I'd come back to square things.'

'Didn't you?'

Gabe shook his head. 'You got enough brains to know why I came back.'

Zac scowled and shifted his glance sideways to his sister. 'Yeah, well, in case you *did* have notions of squarin' anythin' with the Crocketts, you can forget 'em. They're both dead.'

Ronan stiffened. Ellie looked sharply at her brother who smiled crookedly. 'Seems the fools tried to rustle some of Johnny Keyes' cows, but someone caught up with 'em, and there was a gunfight. They shot Ringo and strung up Shep to a cottonwood and I don't reckon Jake Gant is gonna let anyone get away with a lynchin' in his bailiwick.'

They both stared at Gabe. 'When did this happen?'

'While you were s'posed to be wanderin' around in the thickets.'

'Zac! What're you implying?' Ellie was pale now as she stared at her brother. 'You know Gabe was here.' Her voice trailed off and Zac smiled crookedly, shaking his head slowly.

'Chuck brought him in before daylight. He'd've had plenty time to get down from the Crocketts. *And* his Colt was empty, rifle only had two shells in the magazine.'

Ellie looked sharply at Gabe and he frowned. 'I felt real bad in there, almost fell off the horse, fired a few shots trying to attract Chip and Renny.'

'Yes! That must've been the shooting Chuck heard and mistook for a gunfight.'

'Mebbe it *was* a gunfight!' Zac said. 'Between the Crocketts and Ronan: drivin' Key steers on to their land, so's he'd have an excuse to kill 'em both!'

Gabe looked worried now. 'Your cowboy'd need mighty good ears to hear shooting from that high up, anyway, what was he doing out so damn early?'

Ellie spoke up. 'There's been a rogue wolf taking our calves in that pasture just below the slope where Chuck found you, Gabe. Chuck's done a lot of dog hunting and he laid traps and poison baits. He went out early to pick up any unused baits so other animals wouldn't eat them and die.'

Zac laughed. 'Don't look too good for you, does it, Ronan? You ask me, that fever was all a fake.'

'Zac! You're being stupid! I was here; I saw the fever, how it racked Gabe! He has an infected wound!'

Zac shrugged. 'Try and convince Jake Gant: Mitch is just back from town and he said Bill Renny rode in like the devil was on his back and usin' spurs, went straight to the law office. Now Jake Gant's on his way into the valley, askin' about the Crocketts, mad as a hornet. He'll come here, Ronan, might even throw you in jail – with a bit of luck!'

Ellie looked really worried now. Gabe didn't feel very relaxed, either. Zac was the only one of the trio enjoying this. Gabe was weak and his wound was sore, but something surged up in him and with a movement that startled both the girl and Zac, he flung back the sheets, surprised to find he was naked, but not letting it worry him as he said, 'Might be better if I clear out of here before Jake Gant arrives.'

'Oh, Gabe, don't be silly!' Ellie rushed to his side, trying to press him back into the bed but he was strong enough to wrestle her to one side. '*This is plain stupidity! You'll kill yourself!*'

She was emotional and trembling but Zac merely shook his head. 'Relax, sis, He ain't goin' nowhere.'

Dawson came round the bed and lifted his sixgun, waving the barrel under Gabe's nose. He spread a hand against Ronan's chest and thrust him back on to the edge of the bed. Gabe winced and grunted in pain. Ellie tried to pull Zac away without success.

Dawson was scowling now, eyes ablaze. 'You stay put, Ronan! I reckon *you* were the one nailed the Crocketts, not that they're any great loss. But I want to see Gant drag you off to jail! You should never've come back here! And if there's a way of gettin' rid of you, well, hurry on Jake Gant!'

'Zac, leave him be. He – he can't possibly have driven cows up to the Crocketts and fought them in the condition he was in when Chuck brought him here.'

'I say he could!' Zac whirled towards his sister and Gabe acted.

He got both hands on Zac's shoulders and smashed him forward savagely, into the wall beside the bed. The gun clattered to the floor and Gabe rammed Zac's head into the wall again, let the dazed man slump. He was dizzy from the effort but he reached down and scooped up the Colt.

Dawson, semi-conscious, was fighting to get up and Ronan clipped him across the head, bringing a small cry from the horrified Ellie, as Zac spread out on the floor.

'What're you *doing*!' she demanded. 'Gabe, you've hurt him.'

'He's got a hard head.' He sat on the bed panting, a little fresh blood showing at the edge of the bandages covering his wound. 'Ellie, I'm sorry if it's upset you, but I've got to get out of here. You can see how bad it looks, even with you backing my story. It's still possible for it to have happened the way Zac said. No! Don't look like that! I might've been half out of my head with fever, but I damn well know I never even saw the Crocketts. But Jake'll want *proof*! Will you get me some of Zac's clothes? And my own guns, and I'll need to borrow a horse.'

She stood there looking at him blankly, small hands knotted into fists, making up her mind about this. Then she glanced at Zac who was starting to snore and she drew down a deep breath and nodded jerkily.

'All right! I did you wrong seven years ago, Gabe, I hope this will help make up for it.'

'Ellie, just hurry it along, OK?'

Her eyes narrowed and then she nodded and hurried from the room.

He sat on the bed, breathing hard, one hand rubbing his side just beneath the bandages. The last thing he felt like was leaving here and running. He knew how bad it would look but he had no choice.

Seemed everyone was right: he should never have come back here.

It had almost been more restful in jail, halfway to hell!

CHAPTER 12

WHERE'S GABE?

Johnny Keyes lit his cheroot with a series of deliberate movements, not exactly slow motion, but more
like a ritual.

Seated across from the rancher in one of the
uncomfortable office chairs, Chip Allard, trail-
grimed, clothes ragged, eyes reddened, knew
Keyes was not happy with the news he had brought
him.

Johnny blew a plume of smoke, examined the
glowing tip of the cheroot and only then did he turn
his head and look directly at Chip. 'I only wanted
him lost temporarily. Where the hell is he now?'

Allard shrugged. 'Told you, I dunno. Both Renny
and me went lookin' for him right after dark when
he didn't come back from the thicket. Hell, we were
lost ourselves for a while! Nary a sign of Gabe,
Johnny. He musta got out somehow.'

'It was probably the worst place you could've sent

him.' There was censure in Keyes' words and his face was hard.

'All you said was to *lose* him. It was the closest place to do just that. We never had time to go traipsin' all over the Hotspurs to find a place that'd suit Mr Gabe Ronan!'

Johnny Keyes swung his chair around to face his ramrod squarely now. He drew deeply on his cheroot and peered through the smoke. The seconds dragged on. Chip stirred.

'I wanted him lost but not so bad he couldn't find his way back. I wanted to see how he did it, how long it took him, see if he'd lost the old touch, or was just as good as he used to be. I needed a picture of the man! If he's after me, I want to know just what I'm up against!'

'Johnny, I figured he wouldn't go far when he saw how thick it was in there. I was damn sure that blamed sorrel wouldn't move an inch into the thorn thicket but . . .' He shrugged, speading his big, work-calloused hands, the palms showing mild rope burns. 'I dunno where he coulda got to. I try to do what you want, Johnny. You know that.'

'And then some, lately! You don't seem as friendly to Gabe as you were. You figure he's still in the thicket?'

'I dunno. We were lookin' for him when we heard all this shootin' upslope. I knew it was comin' from the Crocketts and I wondered if they were drunk enough to try hittin' our herds on the high graze. Or, if Gabe'd slipped past us and gone after 'em. So we rode on up.'

'And found Shep swinging from a rope, Ringo shot to death.' Keyes' eyes narrowed thoughtfully. 'You think it could've been Gabe?'

Chip Allard looked uncertain. 'He *could've* slipped by us. It was his new rope round Shep's neck. Gabe might've driven some of our cows on to Crockett land, then went after 'em.'

'The cows were his excuse to jump Shep and Ringo?'

Chip nodded firmly now. 'Looks that way. It's the kind of crazy thing Gabe'd do when he's riled.'

'Seven years ago he might've. But if he's riled at the Crocketts, then he's riled at all of us. Think about that?'

'Well, Gabe never was one to let you all the way into his thoughts, Johnny, you know that. Thing is, he – he's kinda entitled to be mad at us all, ain't he?'

Keyes smoked silently. Then, 'S'pose he did drive our cows on to Crockett land and nail 'em, where the hell is he?'

Allard shrugged again. 'Beats me. I mean, Renny and me thought he was still in the thicket, which, of course, would be a good alibi for him if he was the one killed the Crocketts! He could say he never found his way out.'

Keyes said nothing, frowning.

'Well, one place we know he didn't go was the Dawsons,' Chip said. 'That thicket goes most all the way down to Dawson land out there, but Zac'd shoot him on sight.'

'Yeah, no love lost between 'em. But if Gabe came out of the thicket, hurt, needing help?'

Chip shook his head. 'Zac wouldn't help him. Hates his guts. I sent Renny in to tell Jake Gant about the Crocketts. I bet the last place Jake checks is the Dawsons'.'

'I'd like to see Gabe before Gant catches up with him,' the rancher said, tight-lipped. 'Get this Crockett thing cleared up between us, see if he *is* out to get us all.'

'Well, I don't like to say it, Johnny, but I figure now Gabe did kill the Crocketts. I reckon he *is* after us. Gant's no fool, a pain in the ass, but no fool. He'll soon figure if Gabe's guilty or not, then our worries are over.'

'That make you happy, Chip?' Keyes asked quietly, eyes penetrating. 'You *want* to see Gabe in trouble again?'

Allard pursed his lips. 'I like Gabe, but I know how tough he is and if he's comin' after us, well, I'd just as leave he was locked away or swingin' from a rope somewhere. I sure don't fancy goin' up agin him in a square-off.'

'You're pretty tough yourself, Chip, why I gave you the ramrod's job and why you'll run this place when I get the Judgeship. I'm with you in not wanting to have to trade lead with Gabe Ronan, but he's got a lot to square away if he's so inclined. I'm just not sure that's why he's here. I think he really came back for the girl.'

'Ellie Dawson? Judas, Hank said she nearly tore his eyes out in the livery! He might've come back for her but I bet she ain't been waitin' on him.'

'Women are funny.' Johnny heaved out of the

chair. 'All right, we'll wait for Jake to show up, I guess, and where's Renny? He ought to be back.'

'I told him he could have a few beers in town first if he wanted. He's riled at Gabe for not payin' him for his lariat and I thought it'd smooth him over.'

'Damnit, why'd you do that? Renny's mean when he's got likker in him! You *trying* to stir up more trouble?'

Chip shrugged. 'Another man agin Gabe won't hurt, Johnny.'

Keyes stared coldly. 'Won't hurt who?' he gritted. 'Thought Gabe was your friend.'

Chip looked uncertain, then his jaw hardened.

'I don't have friends who're tryin' to kill me.'

Now that Gabe had quit the Dawsons he wasn't sure where to go. Johnny Keyes might take him in again, but if Jake Gant showed, that would put Johnny on the spot with the law: turn Gabe in or lie and say he hadn't seen him.

Besides, there was something just a little queer about the way Chip had sent him into that thicket where he became lost so easily. If he hadn't been in the grip of fever he likely would have turned around and back-tracked as soon as he saw how impenetrable the timber and brush was. But, half out of his head, desperate for water, he had continued on. Finally it was the horse that saved him, tearing itself up in the process.

Zac Dawson was right: there wasn't any way that Sheriff Jake Gant would stand for a shooting and lynching in his bailiwick. And if Jake figured Gabe was the one behind it, he was in for some jail time while Jake investigated. Best thing he could do was get out of the valley for a while. He knew the country pretty well between here and Tolliver and he would be out of Providence County. Maybe that wouldn't stop Gant, and it wouldn't look so good running away, but he needed time to try and figure things out.

As long as there was just a possibility he might have gone to the Crocketts, out of his head with fever, fighting mad, he was in more trouble than he could shake a stick at. *And* he had two black marks against him already: he was fresh out of jail, and everyone figured he had a grudge against the Crocketts, and others in the valley. So he cut across the southern part of the Key ranch, making into the hills he would have to negotiate on the way to Tolliver.

He was about halfway there when a rifle crashed from the rimrock of a cutting he was riding through. The bullet ricocheted from some shale a yard to his left and about as far in front. Some of the rock chips stung the horse's forelegs and the animal danced, whinnying.

Those jerky, sudden movements saved Gabe's life as the second shot whined past his head. The jarring hurt his aching body but he slid the rifle out of its scabbard, even as he wheeled the chestnut Ellie had loaned him into a cleft in the rocks. A third bullet hammered and buzzed from wall to wall of the narrow cleft and by then Gabe was slipping out of the saddle, crouching beside a slab of rock. The gunsmoke gave away the bushwhacker's position. Gabe, heart hammering, breathing hard, waited, cartridge in the breech, palms sweaty against the rifle stock.

He glimpsed a patch of colour up there, a shirt sleeve or hat, and instantly the Winchester came up and blasted, two shots close together, the echoes rolling into one. Rock dust spurted and he heard a man's startled yell. There was floundering up on the rim. A man's shoulder appeared as he fought for footing. Ronan shot again and the man slammed back into the rock, bounced forward. His rifle was knocked from his grip and tumbled down into the cutting, exploding and leaping once.

The wounded man hung with one arm dangling over the edge and Gabe, smoking rifle cradled ready, eased up for a better look. It was Bill Renny. He was hurt, writhing, trying to get at his sixgun: he was lying on his right side, pinning the gun in the holster. Gabe lunged for his mount without much thought, wheeled it, and spurred through the short, narrow cutting, slid around a clump of juniper and rode up to the rimrock.

Renny's grey was ground-hitched off to one side, whinnying worriedly as Gabe quit leather and ran forward just in time to kick the Colt from the cowboy's hand. Renny fell back, his long, stubbled face grey with pain and maybe a little fear. There was blood all over his left arm and side, the shirt red and sodden.

'The hell you trying to do, Bill?' Gabe demanded, breathing hard, fighting his own pain. 'What you trying to kill me for, you son of a bitch?'

'Gant wants you brought in.'

'Never had you tagged as a bushwhacker, Bill,' Ronan said angrily, looking at the man's wound. 'You're bleeding plenty but whatever you got, you asked for.'

'Go to hell!' Renny gritted, struggling weakly as he tried to tear off his neck bandanna. He couldn't manage it.

'Aah, let me see.' Gabe propped his rifle against a rock, brushed Renny's fumbling hand aside and unknotted the neck scarf. Before he wadded it over the gaping wound, he cut Renny's shirt off with his claspknife, wrapped it around the man's body over the kerchief, then used Renny's trouser belt to strap it all in place.

'That'll slow the bleeding some. Wound's deeper than I thought. Bullet's still in there, I reckon. Where is Gant, by the way?'

'Right behind you!' a voice snapped, simultaneously with the clash of a rifle's lever working. 'Just step away from that Winchester and lift your hands, Gabe. You try anythin', I'll shoot your legs out from under you!'

Gabe obeyed slowly, lifting his arms with an effort. He knew he was in no shape to try and outwit Jake Gant.

'I didn't kill the Crocketts, Jake.'

'We'll see. Keepin' a cell warm for you, Gabe, and this time you better get ready for a long stay. I've given you all the breaks I can. From now on, it's strictly by the book and so far the book shows you're well and truly in the red.' Gant allowed himself the beginning of a smile. '*Blood* red!'

'Oh, very funny!' gasped Renny, holding a red hand over the sodden bandage Gabe had put around his wound. His belligerence had gone now and he was beginning to show some fear. 'Never mind *his* blood. I'm the one leakin' like a hog with its throat cut!'

Gant took a look at the wound, and pursed his lips. 'You did a good job, Ronan. Looks like the bullet clipped an artery, cut a vein at least. Sooner we get you to a doctor the better, Renny. But it'll be a rough ride and you're gonna lose a lot more blood. Nothin' I can do about it; you'll just have to take your chances.'

Bill Renny licked his lips. 'Wish I'd never heard of you, Ronan! Or the goddamn bounty!'

'Bounty?' queried Ronan, puzzled.

But the sheriff roughly grabbed Gabe by the shoulder. 'Turn round, hands behind your back,' he snapped.

Gabe obeyed and winced as the lawman snapped the manacles on his wrists. Jake shoved him roughly towards his chestnut and he turned his head over his shoulder and asked,

'You got a bounty on me already?'

'Not me,' Jake said indifferently. 'C'mon, I'll give you a hand to mount. And here's somethin' else for you to think about. If Renny doesn't make it, it'll be another dead man down to you. You're diggin' your own grave, boy. Fast and deep.'

Jake grunted as he heaved Gabe up awkwardly and Ronan settled uncomfortably in the saddle. He looked down at the sheriff, seeing the man pressing a hand into his wounded side. It must have hurt to manhandle a man like Ronan, muscles stretching and straining over that wound as he worked to get Gabe into the saddle.

'If you didn't put a bounty on me, who the hell did?' Gabe asked, but by that time the sheriff was busying himself with Bill Renny and he didn't bother to answer.

Gabe frowned deeply: whoever had put that price on his head had made him into a walking target.

The odds were great for anyone who could afford a five cent bullet to kill him, then collect five-hundred *dollars*.

He had no doubt there would be plenty of takers.

CHAPTER 13

GONE!

The doctor came back into the room where he had insisted the sheriff wait and although he knew the lawman was eager for news about Bill Renny's condition, he indicated a narrow, high bunk.

'Climb on up, Sheriff. Don't look at me like that! It's time I inspected that wound of yours.' He rolled up his sleeves, washing his hands in a basin of cloudy water that smelled strongly of chlorine.

Gant sighed, seated himself on the edge of the bunk and unbuttoned his shirt. As Doctor Dundee loosened the bandages Jake sucked in a sharp breath. The sawbones raised his eyebrows briefly, kept peeling the bandage back.

'How's Renny? He gonna make it?' Gant asked.

'He's dying.'

'What!' Jake stiffened but the medic smiled thinly. 'He was hit pretty bad but I didn't think he was dyin'.'

143

'It's what he believes, though, and I don't seem to be able to dissuade him.' Dundee straightened, throwing the dark-blooded pad into a waste bin, then went to a cupboard for more lint and a pair of scissors. 'It's coming along nicely, Jake. If you'd rest up as I prescribed, it'll be healed in a few more days.'

'That's fine with me,' Gant said, dismissing it. 'But if Renny's dyin', I need to talk with him, Doc.'

'He's not dying. He's lost a good deal of blood, certainly, but it's not that critical. He's feeling bad, and shock is setting in with some depression. Probably pull himself together in a day or so.'

Gant watched as the new pad was bandaged over his newly cleaned wound. 'But right now, he's convinced he's dyin' . . . that right, Doc?'

The sawbones frowned, nodding a mite irritably. 'I believe I told you that two or three times in the last few minutes, Sheriff. I'll have another talk with him this afternoon, convince him otherwise.'

Gant's hand went out and grabbed the thin arm. Their eyes met. 'Doc, like you to do me a favour.' The medic stared back levelly, waiting. 'Let me see Renny before you go boostin' him up, OK?'

'You want to speak with him while he's in this state of depression?'

Gant, buttoning his shirt, smiled. 'Can't think of a better time to do it. What d'you say, Doc?'

They came after dark as Gant had known they would. He had heard the din in the bar of the Pink Lady growing louder during the afternoon, the shouting and cheering, all slurred as the liquor flowed. Once

144

there was a gunshot and Gant was halfway out of his chair without even thinking about it. Then he slumped back down, forcing himself to stay put. No sense in nipping things in the bud just yet, let it happen, then grab the ring-leaders.

Gant's wife cooked an early supper for Gabe Ronan who had slept the afternoon away in his cell. The sleep had done him a lot of good and he felt ready for almost anything.

Almost.

But not quite the news that Gant brought him as he slid the supper tray through the special slot in the bars just before sundown. 'Lynch mob workin' up in the Lady.'

Gabe paused as he picked up the tray of food. 'A *lynch* mob!'

'Mmmm. Bill Renny died, you know. Didn't see the sense in wakin' you just to tell you that you're now gonna be charged with another murder as well as all the other stuff.'

Gabe sat carefully on the edge of the bunk, his appetite suddenly gone. 'Damn! But it was self-defence, Gant! You must've heard the shooting in that cutting, even if you didn't see the last part. Renny bushwhacked me. Still not sure why. He reckoned I owed him money for a saddle-rope, but,hell, it had to be more than that.'

'Renny was OK but he could be a hardcase when he got riled. Or needed money. And he was always broke.'

'Yeah, he put the bite on me for that rope. But he

was out of luck.'

'Seems he left a wife somewhere back east with a kid. He has to send 'em money regular or he goes to jail.' Gant paused as he added, 'And there's five-hundred bucks bounty ridin' on you. That might do it.'

'Judas! Yeah, Renny mentioned something, you were there, said you never put a price on my head.'

'Nor I did.'

'Then who?'

Gant took his time and Gabe forked up some mashed potato without even noticing what he was doing. 'I'd guess it was Johnny Keyes. Chip Allard said as much to Renny, he told me.'

Gabe set the tray on the bunk and went to the bars. 'Now why would Johnny? Hell! He's treated me good since I came back, better than the others, come to think of it! I don't think he really believes I've come back to square anything. Johnny took me at face value.'

'Well, Renny said he and Chip Allard were *s'posed* to see you got lost in the Hotspurs. Keyes' orders. You thinkin' any about that?'

Gabe Ronan went back to the bunk and began to eat automatically, something telling him he just might need the extra energy the food would provide. He spoke slowly.

'If I was "lost" at the time someone drove Key steers on to Crockett land, shot Ringo, lynched Shep with the new rope they gave me at the ranch . . .' He broke off, looked sharply at Gant. 'Folk could think *I* did all those things and was claiming to be "lost" as my alibi.'

146

'That's how it looks to me,' admitted Gant. 'You used the Key cows as an excuse to shoot it out with the Crocketts, or somebody did, so you'd be blamed.'

'You know it wasn't me, Jake. I was set-up and, damnit! It points to Johnny Keyes!'

'Your old pard, the man with the most to lose if you talk about who was with you the night Owen Dawson was killed. Just an accusation that Keyes was part of a drunken prank that cost a man his life and didn't own up, it'd end his chance of ever being Chief Judge of Providence County.'

Gabe ate, swallowing, but not tasting any of the good food Mrs Gant had cooked. He was shovelling it in now, unaware of what he was doing. 'And all the time I thought Keyes was the one man who *knew* he had nothing to fear from me.'

Gant shrugged, took out tobacco sack and papers and started making a cigarette. 'Well, I don't reckon you convinced him. He thinks he can't trust you any more to keep your mouth shut. So, with three of your old bunch dead, he's takin' precautions.'

'Why would he think I'd tell now after keeping quiet for seven years? It's all over and done with.'

Again Gant shrugged, tossed the sack and papers and a vesta on to the end of the bunk. Gabe set aside the empty plates, started making a cigarette.

'Decided he can't take the chance. You did seven years hard-time. That can make a man see things mighty differently. Specially when you came back and found Keyes now owns half the valley. He could be forgiven for thinking you'd want some compensation for what you did for him and the others. See,

147

maybe *he* thinks that way and figures everyone else does, too.'

Ronan lit his cigarette and sat back against the stone wall. 'I'd've expected any of them to do the same for me if they'd got caught. We even took an oath on it years ago.'

'Like I said, the years can change a man. He conveniently forgets things that no longer matter to him.'

'If Keyes thinks that way he must be damn pleased to know you've arrested me and that Renny's dead: that's one more mouth closed permanently and just to be sure of things, he's had someone stir up a lynch party!'

'They'll be here in less than a hour, unless I miss my guess. Soon as it's dark.'

'You got deputies?' There was anxiety in Gabe's question.

Gant smiled thinly. 'Only if I hire 'em and pay for 'em myself. I don't get no allowance for permanent ones.'

'You gonna get some to back you up?'

'Missus is expectin' again, and we've had a lot of expenses. Might even have to send her to Denver Hospital this time around, so no deputies.'

Gabe was at the bars now. 'Damnit, Jake! You can't handle a lynch mob alone! How about giving me a gun to defend myself?'

Gant laughed and walked away down the passage. 'Didn't know you were such a comedian, Gabe!'

Ronan's knuckles whitened around the iron bars as the sheriff strolled back to his front office. Gabe swore softly and then, listening, he too heard the building crowd noise coming from the Pink Lady just up the street.

Suddenly, the cigarette tasted like sawdust and he ground it into the stone flags of the cell floor savagely.

Gant had been waiting in his darkened office ever since he had finished speaking with his prisoner. He watched from the front window, standing at an angle so he could see up the street to the saloon, which was on this side.

There were two loaded shotguns on the desk as well as two rifles and two Colts. His own Colt was in his holster and he kept touching it with his hand while he watched and waited, as if making sure it was still there. People were gathering along the board-walk across the street: they knew what all the racket meant. Likely the news had spread through the town before *he* even had a hint of what was going on.

He was about as ready as he could be and he swore for the hundredth time as sweat stung his eyes, rolled down his face. His shirt was soaked with dark wet patches and his palms felt slippery. He'd never faced a lynch mob before.

'Come on!' he gritted, crouching. 'Get it over with!'

The growing sound of mob rule reached him clearly – there was utter silence in the cell block – and only his own heavy breathing disturbed the quiet surrounding him.

Then it started.

The batwings suddenly slapped back and a crush of men spilled out on to the boardwalk. Light glinted off bottles that were held aloft or passed around for last minute courage. It also showed some hands holding guns.

And one man held a coil of rope high.

Someone had done some fast talking to stir up this mob, Gant thought. Bill Renny hadn't been all that popular. He was a likeable enough ranny, sober, but there was a mean streak in him and some of the townsfolk had felt the lash of his tongue, and one or two the thud of his fists when he was throwing a Saturday night wingding. But his 'death' was as good an excuse as any for a lynch party. Free booze made the idea even more attractive. So here they were, ordinary townsmen, bellies full of rotgut, and ready to commit murder, because in Gant's book, that's what a lynching was. 'Justice' didn't enter into it. A court of law dispensed what passed for justice, here or anywhere else in the country. Any man who took part in a lynching was aiding and abetting murder.

These fools didn't realize that, but they were about to find out. *Right now!*

He gathered his guns, set them up on chairs just inside the door and, holding one of the buckshot-loaded Greeners, stepped out on to the law-office porch to confront the lynch mob as it stormed down the street. Men yelled and shouted abuse, all aimed at Gabe Ronan, a man they barely knew: even those who had been here seven years ago when he had been tried and found guilty and sent to Purgatory Penitentiary. They knew he had a reputation for wildness and hard drinking, although the seven years in prison seemed to have toned down those things.

So whoever had whipped up the mob must have painted a pretty bad picture of Gabe Ronan.

They saw Gant now, slowed, and some in the front ranks stepped back and lost themselves in the crush. But there was one man who stayed put, the man who held a coiled rope, the obvious leader.

'Don't be stupid, Jake! We'll stomp you like a buffalo stampede and tear your lousy law office apart if you try to stop us gettin' to Ronan!'

'If he hears your voice, Chip, he sure must be wonderin' why in hell you're such a goddamn turn-coat!'

Chip Allard's face was wild, his eyes staring and hot with passion. He shook the rope. 'I work for Johnny Keyes! Best man ever rode the river! Gabe was a friend, I admit, but he's out to ruin Johnny and I don't aim to let that happen!'

'You're drunk Chip. Go someplace and sober up. Then I won't have to kill you.' Jake lifted the shotgun and Allard tensed, the men around him easing back.

Chip sneered. 'You ain't about to shoot your own townsmen, Jake!'

'How about we let a court of law decide on Ronan, Chip?' Gant still sounded reasonable but he was tensed and alert, trying to watch all the movement in the mob, men leaving, others joining, constant motion in and out of the shadows, demanding plenty of his attention.

'He killed the Crocketts!' Allard yelled. 'Not good citizens, maybe, but men who spent their money in this town, lived their own lives up by the high pass, not botherin' folk down here. But Gabe Ronan figured they'd let him take the rap for somethin' they had a hand in and he decided to square it away. Who's next? Me? Milo Rafferty's already gone!'

'Another upstanding citizen!' Gant said with a sneer. 'You must've worked damn hard to get this riff-raff behind you, Chip, though I guess plenty of free drinks helped.' He cocked both hammers of the Greener. 'But they try to go along with you and this lynchin' and Doc Dundee's gonna have to go without sleep for three days straight, he'll have so much business! So, any you bright fellers want to change your minds and leave, right now's the time to do it!'

A few men took the opportunity to quit while they were ahead. Chip Allard yelled at them to 'stay put'. Gant raked his gaze over the murmuring, milling mob, some still uncertain, and didn't see the stick that whirred out of the darkness and thudded against the side of his head. His knees buckled and the shotgun exploded with a thunder that scattered the mob, the charge of buckshot chewing a huge splintery half-moon out of the edge of the porch.

'C'mon! Get him!' yelled Chip Allard, running forward.

Once they saw the sheriff was out of it for now, dazed, an unloaded shotgun falling from his grasp, blood sliding down his face, they rushed the front of the law office. A couple got in good licks at Gant, remembering rough-ups on Saturday nights when he had literally dragged them off to jail, maybe after bending a Colt barrel over their heads. Gant's body was kicked off the porch and he dropped into the gutter as the van of the mob surged on with a shouting, yelling rush, crowding into the small office.

They overturned the desk and chairs. Someone grabbed a lamp and lit it and Chip Allard took down the ring of keys from above the empty gun case and opened the door leading to the cell block.

'Now, let's get the son of a bitch and swing him from the highest branch of that tree outside!'

Roaring, jostling, they charged down to the cell block, the man with the lantern a few steps ahead. Staggering, he went to the door of the first of the two cells, held the lamp high, but its yellow light only outlined the bars' shadows slanting across an empty, undisturbed bunk.

'Next one, next one!' Chip Allard shouted hoarsely, shoving the man along.

The lamp lifted and the man snapped his head around, jaw sagging. 'It's empty, too, Chip! He's gone!'

Chip Allard's face was ugly and cast in iron as he stomped out on to the porch where the dazed and muddy sheriff was just trying to get to his feet. The mob, some sobering fast now with the let-down of not finding Ronan helpless in his cell, came out of the office, a few sauntering away, others looking uncertain but still staying close. Chip stepped forward and smashed the stiff coils of the rope he held across Gant's head. The lawman sagged to one knee and Allard grabbed him by the throat, shouting into his face.

'You bastard! You stalled us! Put on a show like he was still in the jail and all the time you'd gotten him out!'

He tightened his grip as Gant's hands clawed at the locking fingers cutting off his air. Chip shook him and some of the men tried half-heartedly to pull his arms away.

'Take it easy, Chip! Gant's still our sheriff!'

He rounded suddenly, letting go with one hand, palming up his sixgun. Eyes bulging, he shot the nearest townsman in the leg and the man howled and sat down, gasping. That was going too far for the remainder of the mob. Someone muttered, 'I'm gettin' outta here!' Someone else said they better get the wounded man to a doctor and in no time at all, some carrying the bleeding townsman, all watching Allard warily, the mob was reduced to less than a dozen hangers-on. People across the street began to spread out and break up too, as Chip kept choking Gant, shaking him savagely. Coming after a prisoner was one thing, but roughing up the sheriff, shooting a citizen, that was just too much for most folk: *Chip had gone plumb loco!* A few grim-faced women grabbed their drink-sodden husbands by the ears and dragged them away. And suddenly the street looked mighty empty.

'Where is he? What'd you do with him, goddamnit?' Chip yelled, still shaking the dazed, gagging Gant by the throat.

'He's a – long way – from here,' choked the sheriff and Chip flung the man from him, kicked him in the side as he sprawled. Jake Gant almost passed out. What remained of the crowd disappeared quickly: this was shaping up into the kind of night they wanted nothing to do with. Liquor fumes had clouded their judgement earlier; now the reality of violence had hit home and few remained to back Chip Allard. He raged when he saw his planned lynch-party was rapidly falling apart, and leaned over Gant.

'Damn you, Jake! What've you done with Gabe?'

The Colt came over threateningly and then there was a shot in the night, a bullet whining off the porch edge. Chip jumped away from Gant in fright and others still on the porch scattered. Allard whirled and his eyes slitted as he saw Gabe Ronan standing in the entrance of the side-street between the law office and the livery. There was a smoking Colt in his hand, glinting in reflected lamp-light.

'Here I am, Chip, *old pard!* Or don't that apply any longer?'

Allard was breathing heavily now, aware at last that he now stood alone. He focussed his attention on Gabe Ronan.

'You always did lead a charmed life, Gabe! God-*damn* you! Why the hell couldn't they've hung you seven years ago! Or why couldn't you've died in jail? Christ knows I spent a small fortune trying to arrange it!'

'You did?' croaked Jake Gant holding his aching throat. 'Or Johnny Keyes?'

Chip curled a lip. 'Let's say it was Johnny's money. I did it *for* Johnny and the rest of us: we were the ones with somethin' to lose. Gabe had already lost. Was just a matter of keepin' him quiet. Why should he come back and ruin our lives, too?'

Gabe, frowning, said to Allard: 'You saying all

those times in Purgatory when some of those scum jumped me or tried to roll a boulder on me, put rattlers in my bunk and so on, were *arranged?*' Chip glared, said nothing. 'By *you*! Why the hell, Chip?'

'Yeah, it was me!' Chip told him tightly. 'Johnny knew nothin' about it. "Gabe's all right," he kept sayin'. "Leave him be. If he says he won't talk, he won't." Just 'cause he *liked* you! *I* wasn't gonna take no chances!'

Gabe said quietly, 'Wasn't good enough for you, eh, Chip, Johnny trusting me. Must've given you a shock when he gave me that room at Key, offered me a job. What was it? Worried you wouldn't get to run the spread when he got his Judgeship? Have a free hand with Key? Run it *your* way?'

Chip spat. 'Mebbe. Johnny risked his life for you once, but the rest of us weren't so damn soft! We knew you could be hard as hell's hinges when you wanted to be. And you had plenty to square away this time!'

'That why you tried to stop me on the train?' cut in Gabe, seeing a lot of things now in a new light. 'Fixed it with Red Abbott and his bunch?'

'Well, you surprised the hell outta me when you shot your way out of *that*, I gotta say!'

Gabe smiled thinly. 'Seven years changes a man, Chip. You let Abbott and his men use that linecamp, turned up in time to shoot Red dead before he could spill anything to me. Even made out you were saving my life.'

'You fell for it!' Chip said sourly.

'Never felt easy about it. Then you showed up

when Milo tried for me, put that extra bullet into him just to make sure.' Gabe shook his head sadly. 'It has to've been you and Renny drove the "stolen" steers up to the Crocketts, and killed them, after sending me into that thicket and using my rope to hang Shep. Set me up, then fixed it for a lynch-party.'

'You can't prove a thing, not with Renny dead, and no one to back you.'

'Renny's not dead.'

All eyes turned to Jake Gant as he struggled to a sitting position, rubbing his throat. 'He *thought* he was dying and I persuaded the doc to let him go on thinkin' that. Renny wanted to clear his conscience, Chip, so confessed to the Crockett deal. He's still alive. Says you told him Gabe had a five-hundred dollar bounty on his head, guaranteed to make a man like Renny get Gabe in his sights, I reckon.'

Allard surprised them all. He lunged at Gant, dragged him to his feet as a shield, placed the Colt against his head. 'Someone get my hoss from the livery. Anyone tries to stop me, this town'll need a new sheriff!'

He was looking straight at Gabe Ronan now. Gabe was tensed, still holding his gun, but afraid to try and use it while Jake Gant's life was in danger.

Chip, his plans in pieces around him now, suddenly snarled, 'Ah! I ain't about to let you get away smellin' of roses, Gabe! Damn you to hell! Johnny'll thank me in the long run!'

'No I won't, Chip. Damn you for a fool! You've gone off the rails!' Johnny Keyes, showing signs of

157

hard riding – sweaty, dusty, clothes awry – came into the light, palming up his sixgun, face hard and cold. 'You're through, Chip! Soon as I heard you were stirring up a lynch-mob I rode in.'

'You're the damn fool! I was doin' it for *you*, you ungrateful son of a bitch!' Allard swung his Colt away from the sheriff, firing instantly. Keyes, staggered, dropping his Colt, tumbling awkwardly to the ground. Wild-eyed, Chip whipped his smoking gun towards Gabe who dropped as the few remaining gawking folk scattered. Gant twisted out of Chip's grip despite his injuries and fell to the porch. Allard triggered at Ronan's moving form as Gabe rolled in the dust, spun around on his belly. He planted his elbow firmly as a bullet spat grit into his face, flinched, but forced himself to stay put, eyes open and clear, thumbing the hammer swiftly, the trigger already depressed. *Three shots. In under three seconds.*

All three bullets slammed into Chip Allard. The Key ramrod jerked and twisted, tried to lift his smoking gun to get off one last shot. But he lost balance and toppled off the porch, sprawled in the street, coughing blood before sliding on to his face, unmoving. Gabe waited a moment then got up, holstering his gun, a little blood staining his side. 'Thanks, Jake.'

The sheriff merely nodded as the doctor hurried down the street towards him. 'Looks like you can still count Johnny Keyes amongst your friends, Gabe. You goin' back to Key?'

Before Gabe could answer, Ellie Dawson came

running towards him, her quirt dangling from one wrist. 'I was hoping you'd come back home with me, Gabe!'

'Well, I sure ain't gonna try to make a decision for you on that one, Gabe!' Keyes said, smiling crookedly. 'But you know you've got a job whenever you need it. Hey, Doc! Take a look at this shoulder, will you? I think my collar-bone's bust.'

'Oh, Gabe!' Ellie said breathlessly, tightening her grip on his upper arm as she added, 'Thank God you're all right! That's all that really matters.'

'Thanks for coming, Ellie.'

'*Will* you come back to ZeeDee with me?'

Gabe's eyes turned to Johnny Keyes who waved in the girl's direction, forcing a smile as Dundee worked on his wound. Gabe nodded, caught Zac Dawson's bleak gaze in front of the small crowd that was re-gathering now the shooting was over. He turned to the girl. 'Yeah, I'd like to come back with you, Ellie.'

Zac curled a lip. He spat on the ground, glared at his sister, whirled, and headed for the saloon.

'Don't worry about Zac. He'll come round,' she said, but didn't sound fully convinced.

'Maybe,' Gabe said quietly. Then, after a pause: 'But what the hell? I'm coming with you anyway.'

He grinned as she stared at him, wide-eyed. Then after a moment she smiled back and tightened her arms around him. 'You're right: who cares how Zac feels? Anyway, I own fifty per cent of the ZeeDee. I'm entitled to have my say.'

Jake Gant said, 'Well, it'll be fun sorting that one

out! But, all round, I reckon you've had a pretty good day, Gabe.'

Ronan looked down into Ellie's face. 'There'll be better,' he said and she smiled up into his face.